Praise for the Novels of H.J. Ralles

The Ghosts of Malhado

From the minute Alex hears those fateful words, to the epic ending that will leave you questioning the words on the wind, *The Ghosts of Malhado* offers a tale in the rich tradition of all ghost stories. One of the best young adult reads of the year – **Melody Bussey, *Editor-in-Chief Ghost! Magazine***

Ralles' *The Ghosts of Malhado* offers a winning combination of buried treasure and ghosts from centuries past in a story that will delight young readers.– **Marie Beth Jones, *Former Chairman of the Brazoria County Historical Commission and weekly columnist for the Facts' "Book Beat" and "Tales from the Brazos"***

The Keeper Series

"*Keeper of the Kingdom* is a must read for children interested in computers and computer games. From the first page to the last there is no relief from the suspense and tension. H.J. Ralles has captivated anyone with a fascination for computer games, and has found a way to connect computer-literate children to reading." - **JoAn Martin, *Review of Texas Books***

"H.J. Ralles continues to offer readers a fascinating affiliation between computers and books. Her 'Keeper' stories are wonderful reading experiences."
–*The Baytown Sun*

"Keeper of the Empire is a fun read, with action that grips you from the start. Excellent for middle school and reluctant readers; enjoyable and suspenseful."–**Christie Gibrich**, ***Roanoake Public Library, Roanoke***

The Darok Series

Darok 9 is an exciting post-apocalyptic story about the Earth's last survivors, barely enduring on the harsh surface of the moon . . . An enjoyable and recommended novel for science fiction enthusiasts."–*The Midwest Book Review*

"Darok 9 has the excitement of a computer game, put into a book that parents and teachers will love to see in the hands of their children." –**Linda Wills,** *Rockwall County News*

"If you love a great story, action, adventure, mystery and suspense, you'll love reading *Darok 10*." –**Marsha Barker,** *Assistant Coordinator, Northeast Texas Library System*

To Joe,

Who let the dogs out?

The Ghosts of Orozimbo

By

H. J. Ralles

Top Publications Ltd.
Dallas, Texas

The Ghosts of Orozimbo
A Top Publications Paperback
First Edition

ISBN 978-1-935722-92-2

Also by H. J. Ralles

The Ghosts of Malhado
The Curse of Charron

The Keeper Series

Keeper of the Kingdom
Keeper of the Realm
Keeper of the Empire
Keeper of the Colony
Keeper of the Island

The Darok Series

Darok 9
Darok 10

For Younger Readers

Look Out Of My Window!

www.hjralles.com

Acknowledgements

I would like to thank the wonderful people of Brazoria County, Texas for their help in writing this book. In particular, I would like to thank Michael Bailey and Jamie Murray of The Brazoria County Historical Museum in Angleton, Texas and Suzan Zachariah, my Realtor and my friend.

For

My sons, Richard and Edward

British by birth, but Texan at heart

Orozimbo

As eerie as the moonless night
when hounds once sought revenge,
for Santa Anna's deadly deeds
against our Texan men,
Orozimbo calls to me
through veils of Spanish moss
that hang from old oak trees
along the muddy Brazos.

H.J. Ralles

Contents

Part 1. The Ghosts of Orozimbo

Part 2. The Real Story of Orozimbo

Part 3. Where was Orozimbo?

Part 1

The Ghosts

of

Orozimbo

Chapter 1

Henry slapped his arm. "Darn mosquitoes!"

He flicked off the squished insect, leaving a spatter of deep red blood above his elbow. Where was the bug spray when you needed it? He wasn't enjoying this expedition at all! "Can we please go home now?" he begged his parents.

"Stop complaining and man up!" his father growled. "You're whining like a three-year-old and yet you're thirteen!"

Henry had hiked Texas trails loads of times before and enjoyed every minute, but today was different. This was no state park!

The path was so overgrown that hundreds of stickers stuck to his socks, pricking at his ankles every time he took a step. On either side were tall, gnarled oak trees that had to be several hundred years old. Spanish moss had overtaken their branches. It looked like an invader from another planet, hanging in huge long clumps ready to attack anyone who dared to walk underneath. Henry shuddered. The place was creepy, for sure!

They were somewhere near the Brazos River, in dense underbrush on an old cotton plantation-and for what? His parents had said they had something they wanted to show him . . . something they were excited about . . . something they had dragged him out into this mosquito-ridden place to see-and he hadn't got a clue what it was!

He stopped for a minute and looked over his shoulder-just to check. Check for what, exactly? He didn't know. It was just something he suddenly felt compelled to do. There was not a soul in sight. All he could see was the trail winding into the distance on this isolated land. He wasn't normally scared like this. There . . . he had said it. He was scared!

"Henry, you're lagging again!" his father bellowed. "We haven't got all day!"

"Thank goodness for that," muttered Henry.

He picked up his pace, swatted away more mosquitoes, and tried to push his fear to the back of his mind. What was there to be scared of? This wasn't like him! He was only a few miles from his home in Angleton, Texas and his parents were babysitting him, for goodness' sake!

The Ghosts of Orozimbo

He pulled his iPhone from his back pocket. Yep! There it was-five bars-he even had good reception. This was hardly isolation, was it? So why did he have this uncomfortable feeling in the pit of his stomach?

Red-shouldered hawks circled directly overhead, squawking loudly as if warning him off. Perhaps it was their raucous sound that made the place feel so eerie? He decided that he didn't like this place at all!

Henry stopped dead in his tracks. He felt certain that someone had just breathed on the back of his neck! He turned slowly, his heart racing, unsure who or what he was about to see . . . but no one was there.

"It wasn't the wind," he said to himself. "I know it wasn't the wind because there isn't even a breeze!"

He smoothed his hand round the collar of his T-shirt, feeling even more spooked, and decided not to look behind again. The sooner this hike was over and they went home, the better!

By the time Henry caught up with his parents, he was panting heavily. They were both tall and took long strides. One of these days he'd be able to walk at the same pace, but he still had a lot of growing to do before he would be the same height as either of them. Family members told him constantly that he was the spitting image of his dad at the same age, with thick wavy brown hair, big brown eyes and two large dimples in his cheeks. He hoped that didn't mean that he was also going to lose his hair at an early age like his father!

They approached a clearing and his parents stopped so abruptly that Henry nearly walked on their heels. "Are we done yet?" he moaned.

His mother drew in a deep breath and placed her hands across her heart. "There it is! Just look, Henry! It's Orozimbo!"

She sighed, as if she had seen something magical.

"Oro -what?" Henry asked, standing beside her.

"Orozimbo," she repeated. "Isn't it wonderful?"

Henry stared in utter disbelief at the dilapidated cottage ahead, his mouth hanging wide open. That gigantic pile of rotten wood? His mother thought that was wonderful?

"You're joking, right?" he laughed, squishing another mosquito on his leg. But then he looked at his mother's expression and realized she was completely serious.

"This is what we've walked all this way to see?" he asked. It was the most ramshackle building he had ever laid eyes on and was only fit to be torn down.

"Take a good look around you, Henry. Can't you see the potential here?" his father asked in a business tone.

Henry looked again. "Uh . . . no," he replied

4

honestly.

Was he missing something? The roof had caved in long ago and he could just about make out four white crumbling walls and a couple of window frames. As for the heavy wooden front door . . . it seemed to be standing completely unsupported!

"This is a great investment project," said his father with a satisfied grin.

Henry was speechless. This was one of his parents' dumber ideas, for sure. Project? This was a lifetime's work! "If you're thinking of buying this place, I think we should look elsewhere," he said decisively.

His mom bit her lip and looked disappointed. She sighed deeply again and turned to face him. "Actually, Henry, we've already bought it."

"You've what?" said Henry, gulping. He turned to look at his father for confirmation. "Seriously, Dad?"

"We signed the final papers yesterday. This lovely cottage, along with 43 acres of land, is ours!"

"Lovely cottage? You've got to be kidding me!" Henry was in disbelief. "And what do we want with 43 acres?"

His father folded his arms across his chest and looked proudly at his acquisition. "We'll have cattle . . . and we'll grow things!"

Cattle? This gets worse! thought Henry. What does he know about raising cattle?

5

"The property is set right on the Brazos River with nearly a mile of waterfront and it has an amazing history," his father continued. "This will be a great home when it's renovated! You'll love it when it's done."

"And when exactly will that be?" asked Henry, "Twenty years from now?" He was really struggling with this whole idea.

"Oh, Henry! Don't be so negative!" scolded his mother. "We've already financed the project and had plans drawn up by an architect. We'll show you later this afternoon after we've met with the builder."

His father draped his arm across his shoulder. "The house should be finished before you go back to school in the fall. We can hunt and fish together and we'll get you a four-wheeler. Think of the fun you'll have exploring with your friends and swimming in the Brazos."

"Yeah, water snakes and all," groaned Henry.

His mother frowned, transforming her normally pretty face into something that Henry thought resembled a shriveled apple.

"That's enough, Henry! I like it even if you don't!" She grabbed his father's arm and led him excitedly towards the cottage-or what was left of it.

Henry was still in shock. He stood there, getting eaten alive, watching his parents wading through a sea of weeds, happy and carefree like a pair of kids. What had possessed them to buy this place?

"We'll be down here a lot this summer, Henry, so you'd better get to like it!" his mother shouted over her shoulder.

"Great," muttered Henry when they were out of earshot. "This is really where I want to spend my summer vacation."

"Go-o-o-o awayyyyyyy!"

"What, Mom?"

Henry stared at his parents in the distance . . . no, it didn't seem that the voice had come from either of them-they were totally engaged in their exploration!

"Go-o-o-o awayyyyyyy!"

"Who's there?" Henry asked. He could have sworn he'd heard someone calling! He turned frantically in circles. But he was definitely alone.

"Go-o-o-o awayyyyyyy!" Yes, there it was again! Someone seemed to be saying 'Go away'-and it was coming from the tall bushes to his right!

Henry swallowed hard. The bushes shook violently. Yes, something was definitely in the bushes!

He thought of putting his hand through the gaps in the branches and feeling around, but then thought better of it. What if there were snakes in there? What if someone grabbed him? His heart pounded. He stood staring at the bushes, wondering what he should do.

"Don't be such a chicken!" he reprimanded himself. "I was probably imagining it!"

He inched closer, leaned forward, and slowly parted some of the branches with his arms. Then he mustered up the courage, took a deep breath and stuck his head into the bush.

Two huge piercing blue eyes stared back at him.

"Ahhhh!" Henry said as he leaped backwards!

"Henry!" his father yelled, running towards him. "Are you okay? What on earth are you doing?"

Henry faced his father, who was still panting heavily. "Uh . . . I thought I saw a snake . . . or something," was all he could think to say.

His father sighed. "Well, then, sticking your head into a bush wasn't such a sensible idea, was it?"

Henry shook his head. "I guess not."

His mom caught up. "Just look at your face! You're all scratched up! What possessed you to do that? You know there are rattlers around here!"

She went on and on and on at him in her usual tone. He stopped listening. "Yeah, sure, Mom," said Henry.

"Let's go back to the car," his father announced. "We're meeting with Mrs. Zachariah and the builder after lunch."

The words were like music to Henry's ears. He

sighed with relief. Thank goodness the expedition was finally over!

His parents set off back down the trail at a cracking pace. He took a few steps after them and then paused and turned to take one last look at the pile of debris that his mom lovingly called Orozimbo. Perhaps he hadn't given the place a real chance. Henry shook his head in dismay. "Nah, it's just a heap of junk."

A cold chill came over Henry. He shuddered and turned back to follow his parents-but he couldn't! Inches from his face, glaring at him with big icy blue eyes was a tall, gangly teenager with a gun-and the barrel was aimed directly at Henry! His head was a bizarre distorted shape, his complexion ashen white, and his cold eyes seemed to cut right through him. Henry wanted to scream-but nothing came from his mouth!

He swallowed hard and saw that the young man was strangely dressed in a wide-brimmed brown hat and a suede jacket with a fringed cape. The gun looked similar to the rifles Henry had seen in pictures of Davy Crockett or William Travis at the Battle of the Alamo. Henry's heart raced faster. Instinctively, he raised his arms in the air in a gesture of surrender.

"I told you to go away," the young man whispered in a breathy voice.

"Y . . . y . . . you . . . did?" stammered Henry, feeling sick to his stomach.

"But you don't scare easily, do you?"

Henry was shaking. "D . . . don't . . . don't shoot!"

The young man lowered his weapon. "I want you off this property!" he whispered again.

Henry found himself whispering back, "But . . . I . . . I . . . I'm your friend . . . I'm not your enemy." He wasn't really sure what he was, but he hoped the boy would believe him.

His head felt heavy, as though he were floating through time and space and couldn't get back to reality. Who was this armed teenager and where did he come from?

"That's good then, Henry, because right now you are standing on my property!"

"I . . . I . . . I am?" Henry asked.

"I want you and your family gone!"

"You do?"

"So do not come back!" the young man suddenly yelled, thrusting the rifle toward Henry. "Do you understand me?

"Why?" asked Henry.

"This is my plantation! Don't come back, Henry . . . or you will regret it! Good-bye!"

"Wait! How do you know my name?" shouted Henry, but the young man's image began to fade right before his eyes. Henry reached out to touch him. "Wait! Don't go!" he said a second time, but it was too late. His fingers wafted though thin air. The teenager had already gone.

Henry stared at the path and then at the bush. He felt dazed. He could have sworn he had just seen a young man . . . but if he was real, where was he now? How could he just disappear? And why was he dressed as if he'd just been at the Battle of the Alamo?

Henry recalled the threat. Don't come back . . . or you will regret it! His heart beat faster. He decided he didn't ever want to see the armed young man again! Suddenly he found himself running . . . down the trail after his parents . . . faster than ever before . . . running away from Orozimbo.

Chapter 2

Henry paced back and forth on Mrs. Zachariah's front deck in the heat of the day. She was their realtor and his parents were inside her beach house with the builder discussing the renovation of Orozimbo. They were completely sold on transforming a pile of rotten wood in the middle of 43 acres of spooky mosquito-infested, wasteland into their new home. He hated the whole idea of moving onto Orozimbo, but there was not a darn thing he could do to stop the project!

He slumped down in a beach chair and looked out over the inland waterway towards all the chemical plants, but he couldn't switch his thoughts away from the morning's scary experience. What exactly had he seen? He had tried to figure it out in the car on the way over here. Had he really met a young man with a rifle? Or was it just his intense dislike of Orozimbo that caused his imagination to run wild?

"Nah . . . he was real enough," said Henry, gripping the arms of the beach chair. "As real as Orozimbo."

He could feel sweat on his forehead-and it wasn't from the hot weather. He was freaked out by the thought of spending a large chunk of his summer at Orozimbo! He was even more freaked out by the young man's threatening words. What if he ignored them? Would the young man return with his rifle? What would he do to Henry and his family?

Henry had asked his parents over lunch if they had seen anyone else on the trail at Orozimbo. They had shaken their heads and looked at him in a concerned way.

"Orozimbo is private property, Henry," said his father. "Who do you think we're likely to see on the plantation?"

"Are you feeling okay, Henry?" his mother had asked, touching his forehead with the back of her hand.

Feeling okay? No, he wasn't feeling okay! But he couldn't tell them that.

Henry needed to talk to someone. He thought about texting his best friend, but David was in Europe on vacation for several weeks. Then he thought about texting his cousin, Emily . . . but what exactly would he say in a text? "Hey, Em . . . I've just been threatened by an armed teenager . . . help!"

Mrs. Zachariah came out on deck and handed Henry a bottle of water. She put her sunglasses on and said, "Whew! It's hot out here, Henry! You're welcome to come inside and listen to the exciting plans for Orozimbo."

Exciting plans? Hardly. "Nah, I'm fine, thanks."

"Are you sure? I'm afraid we'll be a while longer," said Mrs. Zachariah.

"That's okay. There's plenty to see from up here."

"Why don't you go down to the Surfside Beach town hall and look around? It's only just over there-it's the large white structure with a red roof." She pointed down the street. "There's a great little historical museum upstairs."

Henry smiled at her. He wasn't really a fan of history and museums, but right now he was prepared to do anything to forget the morning's experience. "Thanks, Mrs. Zachariah. I'll take a look."

"Okay. I'll tell your parents where you are, and they can pick you up when we're done."

Henry headed down the beach house steps and hit the road. He ambled along, breathing in the sea air and watching the gulls squawking overhead. There was a pleasant breeze here at the coast. The flag outside the town hall was fluttering madly, causing a clanking sound as the ropes hit the flagpole.

Henry sat on the red steps of the town hall and opened the bottle of water. He looked up at the white wooden structure and decided that he liked the green railings along the steps and the deck. They matched the trim round the front door and somehow made the building feel welcoming. But did he really want to go inside and learn about history? He sighed. It wasn't his thing. If someone had told him there were video games inside, he'd have been up those steps in a flash!

"You look bored," said an old man who was coming down the steps.

"A bit . . . maybe," said Henry, looking up at him. He squinted in the sun, but it was still hard to see the old man's face, especially as he didn't have any sunglasses.

"I'm Charlie," the man said, extending his hand.

"I'm Henry."

The old man smiled. "Pleased to meet you, son! Are you a visitor to our great little city of Surfside Beach?"

Henry nodded. "We live in Angleton. This is just a day trip," he replied, wishing the day would be over already. "My parents are visiting with our realtor right now."

"Suzan Zachariah, no doubt-she's the best!" Charlie pointed to her little white house on tall green poles.

"You know her?" asked Henry, shielding his eyes to try and see Charlie.

"Sure! I've lived here most of my life and I volunteer at the museum." He motioned to the upper floor of the building. "So I know everyone around here."

"Oh," said Henry.

"Why don't you go inside the museum?" suggested Charlie. "There are lots of exhibits to see, and it's free."

"I'm afraid I'm not really a fan of museums and history."

Charlie chuckled. "That's because you haven't found a connection yet! You wait and see, Henry, young man. Something will happen to get your interest and you'll be hooked on history before you know it!"

"You think?" said Henry, taking another drink of water.

"Sure!" he replied.

Charlie stepped down a step and now Henry could see him clearly. He was a well-rounded elderly man with a short white beard and wisps of white hair that crept from underneath his cap.

"You see, Henry, history is all about our

17

connections with the past, whether it is a connection with people or a connection with a place," said Charlie. "Once you find yours, you'll dig deeper and deeper. By the way, there's a great historical museum in Angleton, right where you live, if you ever need it."

"Thanks, I'll remember that," said Henry, although he didn't think he'd ever set foot in the building.

"So young man, have you read the plaque?"

"What plaque?"

"Over there, on that huge pink granite stone."

Henry didn't dare admit to the old man that he hadn't even noticed it. He turned to look. The black stone with pink flecks was enormous-at least five feet high and probably as wide. It was really a giant boulder with a strangely shaped chunk taken out of the top, as if someone had taken a bite. The boulder was right next to the steps where they were sitting. He couldn't believe he hadn't even seen it.

"Take a look!" said Charlie. "You never know, you might find that connection I was talking about."

Henry glanced towards Mrs. Zachariah's house. His parents' new white Ford Explorer was still parked underneath and so was the builder's truck. He might as well take a look at the stone. He had nothing else to do.

He got to his feet, stepped down onto the sidewalk and followed the old man who was already standing in front of the boulder. It was an amazing piece of granite, for sure, and he could appreciate that since he enjoyed earth science. He rubbed his hands over the rough surface, marveling at its enormity. On the front was a bronze plaque that marked important events.

"'The Battle of Velasco was fought here June 26, 1832,'" Henry read aloud. "June 26-that's today's date!"

"Indeed it is," said Charlie. "What a coincidence."

"'Public and secret treaties of peace between the Republic of Texas and General Santa Anna were signed here May 14, 1836,'" Henry read aloud. He traced his fingers over the raised bronze lettering. "General Santa Anna. I learned about him in school."

"Then you know that General Antonio López de Santa Anna was an important character in both US and Mexican history," said Charlie. "And he was especially important to us here in Texas. First of all, he was responsible for our defeat at the Battle of the Alamo, but then we captured him a month later after a victory at the Battle of San Jacinto. That took place not far from here."

"Wasn't the general hiding in the marsh dressed in a corporal's uniform when the Texans found him?"

Charlie smiled widely, flashing several gold teeth. "So you did listen in class-a little!"

"Just a little," Henry laughed. "I never really cared

about what the teacher was saying, but somehow, today it seems like a pretty cool story."

"That's because you are here on the same day of the year that the battle took place. And you are standing on the very spot where the Treaties of Velasco were signed after that battle. It is exciting because this is where Texas Independence began, and now it feels real to you."

"But if the treaties were signed right here, how come they were called the Treaties of Velasco and not the Treaties of Surfside?" Henry asked.

"Velasco was the first capital of Texas, and Velasco was renamed Surfside Beach 167 years later."

"Oh!" said Henry. "Now I get it!"

Charlie patted him on the shoulder. "You see, history is fascinating. Most people can tell you about those two important battles in our Texas history, and the fact that Santa Anna was president of Mexico numerous times. But there is so much fascinating information that most people never ever learn about Santa Anna. He was a very colorful character. Mostly we hear all the bad things about him, but there were also some good things."

"Like what?"

"Ah!" Charlie chuckled. "I've got you hooked! And that's where I'm going to stop today. Now it is up to you to find out more!"

"Aww!" moaned Henry. "I was just getting interested!"

"Exactly," said Charlie. "You know, I have a feeling that you have a connection with Santa Anna!"

Henry looked at him quizzically. "Me? Really? Why?"

"Just something in my old bones tells me that. Keep digging, my boy. You never know what you might find! Gotta go. It was nice talking to you!"

"Before you go, can you answer a question for me?"

"Sure. Name it."

"What kind of uniform would the Texans have worn into battle during these times?"

Charlie scratched his beard. "Well, there were many different uniforms in the 1830s and 1840s. The official Republic of Texas army was made up of all kinds of soldiers. Some were regulars but most were volunteers. The regular army usually had light brown uniforms with a double- or single-breasted jacket and a peaked black cap. They would have carried rifles and used cannon."

"Oh," said Henry. "What about a jacket with fringed cape and a wide-brimmed brown hat-kind of like the pictures I've seen from the Battle of the Alamo?"

Charlie looked amazed. "What you are describing was worn by many men who were in the militia. The militia were volunteers who didn't have a proper military uniform. It seems that you did take an interest in class after all!"

Henry smiled at him, not wishing to recount his morning's experience. But now he was really confused. How could he have met a soldier from nearly two hundred years ago? He turned to say good bye, but Charlie was already walking away.

"If you want to hear some more Santa Anna stories, I live in the little yellow house just at the end of the next street," Charlie shouted over his shoulder. "Just make sure you tell your parents that you're visiting me."

"Sure. Thanks, Charlie." Henry watched the old man until he turned the corner and was out of sight.

Henry touched the boulder one last time. He had to admit that he was curious to learn more. Both the soldier he had seen at Orozimbo and now Charlie's talk on Santa Anna had certainly sparked his interest. Texas history had caught his attention twice in one day.

Henry wandered back down the street to Mrs. Zachariah's beach house. The builder's truck was no longer there. Perhaps his parents would be ready to leave? He climbed the steps to the deck, counting each one as he went. It sure seemed a long way up on a hot afternoon.

"There you are, Henry!" said his mother as he walked through the door. "We've just finished talking."

"Come and take a look at the plans," said his father eagerly.

Henry bent over the kitchen table. There was no doubt-from the architect's drawings, the house looked nice. The sketches showed a large two-story rectangular building with a huge raised front porch and a balcony up above on the second floor. The house had wide steps down to the front path and plenty of windows. It reminded him of the plantation homes he'd seen in old photographs. "Yeah, it actually looks very nice," he said to his parents.

His mom beamed, and he knew his comment had made her day after he'd disappointed her earlier. "That's good that you like it, Henry," she said. "We've modeled it on the original Orozimbo plantation home that used to be there back in the 1800s."

His father handed him an old photo. "This is what the original plantation house looked like."

"But the ruins that we saw today didn't look anything like this," said Henry.

"No. What you saw this morning was a cottage that was built on the same site four years after the plantation home was destroyed. A farmer lived in the cottage for years."

"Oh," said Henry. "So what happened to the old plantation home?"

"It was destroyed by a hurricane in 1932," his father finished. "But of course our new Orozimbo will be built to today's hurricane standards, with special hurricane ties to hold the roof down and hurricane-proof windows. The glass in the windows will be able to take an impact up to 130 miles per hour!"

"And of course," his mother added, "the house will be raised a few feet off the ground in case of flooding on the property."

"Wow! It sounds like you've thought of everything." Henry couldn't help but feel impressed. Maybe his parents knew what they were doing after all!

"When we're done it will look just like the original Orozimbo. Just think, we'll have a true connection with the past!"

Henry was stunned. What had Charlie just said? History is all about our connections with the past, whether it is a connection with people or a connection with a place. Once you find yours, you'll dig deeper and deeper. And now here it was: a connection with the past presented to him on a plate.

"I think the Ghosts of Orozimbo will be very happy with that decision!" added Mrs. Zachariah.

"Ghosts?" Henry blurted out. "What ghosts?"

The Ghosts of Orozimbo

"Didn't you know? Orozimbo is rumored to be haunted. There are many stories of ghost sightings on the plantation."

His mother giggled. "Oh, Suzan. You shouldn't fill Henry's head with such nonsense or he'll never want to set foot on the property again!"

"Ghosts! Really!" said his father. "Utter rubbish!"

His parents both laughed raucously.

Henry wasn't laughing with them. He began to sweat profusely. Is that what had happened this morning? Had he actually seen a ghost? That would explain how the young soldier had vanished into thin air right before his eyes!

He looked at Mrs. Zachariah. She wasn't laughing either. In fact, her expression showed complete seriousness and she looked almost upset that his parents thought she was joking.

Henry felt sick. Orozimbo was haunted! What had his parents done?

Chapter 3

Henry sat in the back of the car with a throbbing headache, wishing the day was over. He couldn't believe it-they were on their way back to Orozimbo! What if the soldier returned? Should he tell his parents about how he had threatened them if they came back to Orozimbo? No, it would be pointless. His parents would just laugh and say he had an overactive imagination or was making up excuses to not be there.

"I thought we were going home," he moaned as they pulled up to the wrought- iron gate at the edge of the property. "Can't this wait?"

His mother jumped out of the car, unlocked the padlocked gate and swung it wide open. His dad drove over the cattle grid and onto the crushed concrete drive on the other side while his mother closed the gate behind. She hopped back into the front seat and they continued slowly, bumping down the potholed drive.

Now there was no turning back. Henry felt sick as he looked out of the window.

"We'll be less than an hour, I promise," said his mother. "Now that we have the plans for the house finalized, we want to choose a site for the cabin so that they can deliver it this week."

"What cabin?"

"We're having a cabin delivered so that we can stay up here starting next weekend and oversee construction of the house."

Henry felt even sicker. "We're staying up here from next weekend? That soon?"

They ignored him.

His father stopped the car where the crushed concrete road ended and the overgrown path began.

Henry sighed loudly.

"You can stay here and wait for us, if you like," his mother responded in a conciliatory tone.

"More mosquito bites," he grumbled, getting out of the car.

Henry watched his parents set off down the trail. He longed to go with them, but he was terrified at the thought of seeing the soldier again. He looked around, feeling so vulnerable standing out in the open by the car, but it was way too hot to sit inside the car and wait. No, it was safer to go.

He set off after his parents, swatting away mosquitoes and stopping to scratch his bites. He walked quickly, hesitating by every bush or tree that he passed, half expecting that the soldier might jump out.

Henry reached the clearing and stared at the dilapidated cottage. He tried to visualize a big beautiful plantation home standing on the same spot as the pile of rubble, but it was hard. His parents were already heading away from the clearing, down another trail towards the Brazos River. Despite his mother's assurances, he guessed that they would be over an hour trying to find the perfect spot for the cabin.

He began to relax a little. Ghosts? Nah! There had to be some logical explanation for what he had seen earlier in the day. Perhaps he had been dehydrated and his intense dislike of Orozimbo had caused him to hallucinate? Yes, that had to be it!

So, what could he do to entertain himself for an hour? Should he head down to the Brazos River after his parents? His eyes fell on the crumbling cottage. It seemed to be calling him. He shrugged. Why not explore? He might find something rare amongst the ruins.

Henry waded through the jungle of weeds towards

the cottage, sneezing occasionally. He scrambled over the piles of fallen timbers, being careful not to stab himself on the rusty nails sticking out of some of the planks, and climbed up the concrete steps. The old front door looked so odd, standing on its own surrounded by rubble. Though it was a heavy wooden door, it seemed so flimsy, since it was unsupported on either side. He wondered if it would fall if he pushed it. There was a brass door knocker in the center and a door knob to match. Even though the varnish was peeling off the six panels of the door, showing its age, the brass accessories glistened in the sun and seemed almost new.

Slowly, Henry reached out to touch the brass door knob. He laughed and withdrew his hand. What was he thinking? He didn't need to go through the door at all! There were hardly any standing walls! He could easily walk round either side of the door and into the main room of the cottage. Why risk the door falling on him? But something compelled him to reach out and touch the knob. He turned it slowly and felt it move easily. The door swung open without teetering. It was almost as if there were invisible walls steadfastly holding it up. It had to be bolted to the floor!

Henry stepped over the threshold. He felt suddenly chilled and his vision blurred. A fuzzy image formed directly in front of him and he sensed someone nearby. Everything seemed to be in black and white, making it even harder to tell who or what was there. What was happening? He rubbed his eyes vigorously.

"Help me! Please!" Henry cried, reaching out to take hold of whoever was standing there. "Mom? Dad? Is that you?" He felt someone grab onto his arm and support him. Thank goodness!

Henry's vision cleared and color returned to his sight. His heart raced when he realized that it was the young soldier holding him up upright! He tried to pull away from his grip, but the soldier's hand tightened painfully around his arm.

"Oww! Let go! You're hurting me!"

"Henry!" the soldier said angrily. "I told you not to return!"

Henry was panic struck! With one violent movement he pulled away from the soldier's grasp, tottered about for a few seconds and collapsed on the floor.

The soldier hollered with laughter. The sound reverberated eerily.

Henry looked up at him, shaking with the shock. The soldier's face seemed less scary and ghost-like than before. His complexion was no longer ashen and his face was more rounded. Henry could even see stubble round the young soldier's chin and a few lines across his forehead. Was he a ghost or not?

The soldier had just grabbed him, suggesting that he was a physical being. But on their first meeting the soldier had appeared and disappeared right in front of Henry's eyes! It didn't make any sense.

"How did you know my name was Henry?"

The soldier shrugged. "That's no big secret-I heard your parents call you that." He opened his clenched fist and the rifle flew out of his hand and landed on the floor.

Henry gasped at the sight. He was still trying to comprehend what he had just witnessed when the soldier helped him to his feet.

"Thanks," Henry muttered.

"Why did you did not heed my warning and stay away from Orozimbo?"

"Please, you have to understand . . . I can't control what my parents decide to do. They've just bought this land, so I don't get how you can say you own this place."

"Take a look around, Henry, and you will understand."

Henry turned away from the soldier and studied his surroundings for the first time. He gasped when he realized that he wasn't inside the ruins of the old cottage any longer. He looked up to see dark wooden beams on a high ceiling instead of the clear blue sky. There were no piles of rotten wood and no broken windows or crumbling walls.

Instead, he was standing in a beautiful circular entrance hall with a sweeping staircase that curved up to the second floor. The banister was made of polished wood, and a crystal chandelier that hung from the ceiling cast glistening shapes on all of the walls. On the floor was a deep red woven rug that seemed almost too luxurious to walk on. A large grandfather clock that was positioned prominently by the curve of the stairs suddenly struck 6 o'clock with six loud dongs. Henry jumped.

"Don't mind the clock," said the soldier. "It's been in my family for years."

"Where am I?" asked Henry. "This place is incredible."

"You know where you are."

Henry frowned. What did that mean? "I do?"

"You are in my home."

"Your home?" questioned Henry.

"Orozimbo."

Henry stared at the soldier in disbelief. "But my dad said that Orozimbo was completely destroyed by a hurricane in 1932. Orozimbo has gone."

The soldier's face reddened. The rifle flew off the floor and back into his hands. "Orozimbo will always be here. It will always be my home and it will always stay in my family," he said in an angry tone, stepping towards Henry.

"Er . . . if . . . if you say so," Henry stammered.

"And I will defend it just like I defended Texas from raiding Mexicans!"

Henry was flabbergasted. Raiding Mexicans? He felt fearful once again. He backed towards the door inch by inch, knowing that this whole scenario could have a very bad ending. This was a very angry, armed young man.

"I . . . I . . . think I'd better go," he said as he reached the threshold. He felt for the door frame and grabbed it, still maintaining eye contact with the soldier. With one powerful thrust backwards he just managed to clear the doorframe and throw himself through.

"Oww!" Henry yelled in pain as he landed on his bottom and rolled down the concrete steps onto a large chunk of wood. He looked around. The soldier was gone and he was back in the open air, feeling decidedly hot. The base of his spine hurt and he had a bleeding gash on his knee. But if those were his only injuries, he felt pretty lucky.

"Now what have you done?" shouted his mother as she scrambled over planks of wood to reach him.

"I'm fine, Mom," said Henry, trying not to show he was in pain. "I just tripped."

"Really, Henry! We can't leave you for five

minutes without you getting into trouble! What will you do in a whole summer out here?"

Henry shuddered-if he kept seeing ghosts, he dreaded to think!

Chapter 4

Henry yawned as he gazed into the bathroom mirror. He was still recovering from his escapades the day before and he hadn't slept at all. Ghosts . . . soldier ghosts, in particular, seemed to be all he could think about. He could see black shadows around his eyes, but his parents were so wrapped up in their plans for Orozimbo that they didn't seem to notice. At least he was back home.

He hobbled down the street and knocked on Emily's door. He knew he could count on some moral support from his cousin. She was only a few months younger and a good listener. Emily could always cheer him up when he was feeling down.

The screen door creaked as she opened it. "Hi, Henry. Gee, you look awful!"

At least someone saw that he wasn't himself. "I

feel awful," said Henry as he stepped into her kitchen, which smelled deliciously of freshly baked brownies.

"What happened to you? It looks like you had a fight with a bush-and you're as white as my Halloween face paint!"

"Hey, Em-enough with the jokes," said Henry, collapsing into a seat at her kitchen table. "I know I've got scratches all over my face."

"So you really did have a fight with a bush?" she stifled a laugh.

"Not exactly, but you're close to the truth." Henry lowered his head, rested his elbows on the table and dragged his fingers through his hair. "I had a really bad day yesterday."

"Boy, you really are in a bad way!" Her smile vanished and a deep frown spread across her sun-bronzed face. She grabbed a plate of brownies from the countertop, took two cans of Coke from the fridge and sat down opposite him.

"Here, this'll make you feel heaps better," she said, handing him a plate and a glass full of ice.

Henry pulled the tab on the can and poured out the Coke. He sighed deeply. "Thanks, Em."

"So what's up? I've never seen you so miserable before."

"I know you believe in ghosts, because you've told me that many times," said Henry.

"Sure, I do. What of it?"

"Well, I think I saw one yesterday-twice!"

"For real?" Her whole expression changed from concern to complete awe. "You're so lucky! I wish I had seen one!" She leaned forward to listen, her long blonde braids brushing the table in front of her.

"No . . . you don't! Now I can't sleep and I can't forget about it either. I keep seeing his image in my mind."

"His image?"

"The ghost was a young soldier."

"Wow! Who'd have guessed that your house would be haunted? It's not even old like this one! Maybe it's built on top of a graveyard or something!"

Henry didn't know how to answer that. Her comment almost brought a smile to his face. "No, not my house, Em-Orozimbo,"

"Oro-what?" she repeated, raising her eyebrows.

"I know-it's a mouthful. That's the name of the property my parents have just bought."

"Oh, right. My parents were talking about that last night. I guess your dad had called my dad to tell him he had bought some land. Dad was saying we'd be spending weekends there with you sometimes."

"It's not just any land-it's an old cotton plantation!"

Henry recounted how he had seen the cold blue eyes in the bush and described the young soldier who appeared and disappeared as if by magic.

Emily was so entranced by the tale that she was lying across the table by the time he had finished. "So let me see if I've got this right: the young soldier was dressed as though he'd been at the Battle of the Alamo, in a long fringed jacket and a hat with a wide brim. He pointed a rifle at you and told you that you were on his property, and then he gave you a guided tour of his home?"

Henry couldn't help but laugh. "If you put it like that, it sounds ridiculous!"

"I knew I could get you to smile!"

"But it's all very weird, don't you think?" said Henry.

"Well, not all of it." Her green eyes were wide open with excitement. "If your soldier were a ghost it would make more sense than if he were a person."

Henry frowned. "It would?"

"Sure. What would a person be doing on your private property dressed as if he were at a revolutionary battle and carrying an old-fashioned rifle?"

"Perhaps he's one of those guys that likes to take part in those reenactments of battles that you can go and watch."

They both laughed.

"Nah, I don't think so either," said Henry. "Besides,

my parents would have seen him too!"

"I read a lot about ghosts after I got hooked on that paranormal TV show. Ghosts are usually friendly and usually appear to people who have a connection with them for some reason."

"Friendly? I wouldn't say my ghost was friendly."

"Well, he hasn't really hurt you, has he?"

Henry shook his head. So far it had just been threats. "What do you mean by a having a connection?" That was the fourth time he had heard the word in two days-first from Charlie, then from his mother, then from the soldier ghost and now from Emily.

"Perhaps your ghost used to live on the Orozimbo Plantation, or something?" Emily suggested.

"You think?"

"Sure. That's the connection with you. Your parents are buying the property where he may have lived for years."

"Could be, I suppose," said Henry.

"When are you going back to Orozimbo?" Emily asked eagerly.

"Never, if I have my way!"

"Well, I think you're out of luck. It sounds to me like you're gonna be living there and not just visiting at weekends."

"I know. Mom's already spoken to Mrs. Zachariah

about putting our house up for sale."

"Already?"

Henry nodded sadly. "Hey, Em . . . wanna come and meet a ghost at the weekend?" he half joked.

Emily lit up. "Sure. You know I'd love too!"

"We're having a cabin put on the property this week. It'll only be a small place-just big enough that we can stay there while they build the plantation house over the next few months. Then when the big house is finished, I guess the cabin will be like a guest house."

"Do you think they'll let me come?"

"I can ask," said Henry. "I need a friend with me! I'm honestly sort of freaked out about going back there. I can't tell my parents what I thought I saw. Dad flat out doesn't believe in ghosts and Mom laughed when Mrs. Zachariah talked about Orozimbo being haunted. Mom would take me straight to see a psychologist and have me evaluated!"

Emily giggled. "Yes, she would, for sure." She paused for a moment. "Did you just say that your realtor thinks the property is haunted?"

"Uh-huh. People have reported ghost sightings not only at Orozimbo, but on other property along the Brazos River as well."

"How cool is that!"

"Cool? You think that's cool? I think it's creepy!"

"I know what we should do-we should find out who

your ghost is!"

"And how do we do that? You want me to ask him next time I see him?"

"No . . . the internet, dummy!" Emily grabbed her laptop from the countertop and sat back down at the kitchen table. She opened up Google and typed in Orozimbo Plantation, Texas. "Okay. There's lots of information coming up," she announced.

Henry strained to see across the screen. She angled the computer towards him. Under Google Images there was a photo similar to the one his mother had shown him of the old plantation home. "What does it say?"

"It says that Orozimbo was a cotton plantation owned by a Dr. James Aeneas Enos Phelps and that it was originally over 130 acres but since then some of the land has been sold."

"That's why our Orozimbo is now 43 acres," said Henry.

"Dr. Phelps was born in 1793, came to Texas from Tennessee in 1822, and died in 1847. Do you think that Dr. Phelps was your ghost?"

"Nah, my ghost was a soldier, not a doctor, and he was probably a teenager."

"Dr. Phelps could have been in the Texan army when he was younger."

Henry shook his head. "I don't think it's him. Let's

do the math. If James Phelps came to Texas in 1822 … let's see, that means he would have been 29 years old. My soldier was much younger-I'm guessing 18 or 19."

"It says that Phelps had two sons and two daughters. The oldest son was called Orlando. He was born in June 1822 and-get this-it says he was in the Republic of Texas army!"

"Really? Let me see!" Henry pulled the laptop across the table towards him and read aloud. "The Mier Expedition, November 1842. Orlando C. Phelps served under Captain Charles Keller Reece, Company F. Liberated from Mexico in April 1843."

"If Orlando was born in 1822, he would have been 20 years old when he was in Company F," said Emily. "So when you guessed that your ghost was 18 or 19 years old, you weren't that far off."

"If it's him," said Henry.

"Well, he did grow up there, so it would make sense that he's your ghost."

"It also says Orlando C. Phelps was captain of the Alamo Guard," Henry continued.

"What's the Alamo Guard?"

"Well, Charlie told me that most of the soldiers in the Army of the Republic of Texas were volunteers."

"Who's Charlie?"

"Oh, that's another long story," said Henry.

The Ghosts of Orozimbo

"Anyway, there were lots of volunteer militia units with names like the Milam Guard and the Travis Guard. I'll bet the Alamo Guard was like them. The militia didn't wear a proper military uniform."

"So what did they wear?"

"I think they wore long fringed jackets and hats with wide brims."

"You've just described your ghost!" said Emily.

"I know. It had crossed my mind. And listen to this information-it was written by Orlando Phelps!" said Henry, reading another section. "Attention Militia! The Militia of the Columbia Beat are hereby ordered to attend drill in Columbia, on Saturday next. O.C. Phelps, Captain."

"Where is Orozimbo Plantation?"

"In the city of Columbia," said Henry, feeling very satisfied with their research. "I think you're right. Orlando Phelps is my ghost!"

"He has to be!" said Emily. "Now I can't wait to go to Orozimbo with you. I wonder . . . if we called Orlando by name, do you think he would appear?"

"I'm not sure I really want to find out," Henry replied, although he had to admit that he was quite intrigued by Captain Orlando C. Phelps.

Chapter 5

Friday evening arrived too soon. Henry was still unsure how he felt about returning to Orozimbo, especially now that he knew his ghost was Orlando Phelps.

His mom had been up to the property several times in the week getting the cabin ready. Henry had declined to accompany her and she had been slightly annoyed that he didn't want to come. It wasn't that he was lazy or didn't want to help-just nervous of who might suddenly appear. But he knew couldn't tell her that.

After several days discussing ghosts with Emily and reading about them on the internet, he was almost excited to meet Orlando again.

He had found out that ghosts can touch you. Many

people had posted comments online about ghosts touching their arms or tapping them on the back, so at least he knew that he hadn't imagined being grabbed.

He made a list of five things he had read about ghosts that seemed important.

1. Ghosts usually have unfinished business that they must resolve before they can leave Earth and cross into the light.

2. Ghosts can move objects in an emotionally charged situation.

3. Ghosts can appear anywhere they want to.

4. Ghosts can lower or raise the temperature in small areas.

5. Initially, ghosts' faces often appear to be distorted and scary, but once they start to interact with people they begin to look more lifelike.

Henry had memorized the list and saved some useful web links to his cell phone. He printed off some of the documents, took photos with his cell phone camera, and saved them in his gallery so that he could show Emily later. Everything seemed to fit with his experience. Orlando definitely had some kind of unresolved issue with the ownership of Orozimbo. Henry had witnessed the rifle flying through the air-twice! Orlando had appeared in the bushes, on the trail and in the cottage and Henry had felt cold every time. Lastly, when they had first met, Orlando's face was distorted and it appeared that he was wearing thick white Halloween makeup, but the second time they met, Orlando looked almost human. Henry turned off the power to his cell phone to save the battery.

It was 6 p.m., his parents had already loaded everything into the back of his Mom's silver Explorer, and Emily was eagerly waiting to go. Thank goodness that they were only going to be at Orozimbo for a couple of days this time. Then they would bring Emily home and pick up more supplies.

As he got into the back seat of the car he half expected to see Orlando sitting next to him!

The drive from Angleton to Orozimbo was short. When they arrived at the metal gate, Henry could instantly see that the trail had been widened and cleared by the construction equipment that had brought in the sections of the cabin. He was happier. It seemed less creepy, and now his father was able to drive right up to the edge of the clearing.

Emily leaped out of the car the moment they came to a stop. "Uncle Bill and Aunt Mary, this place is awesome!" she announced, twirling around.

"I'm glad that someone likes it here!" said his mother, giving him a laser-like stare.

Henry groaned. Much as he liked his cousin, she could make his life difficult at times.

They walked past the dilapidated cottage and into

a smaller clearing to reach the log cabin. Overlooking the Brazos River, it seemed welcoming. It had been raised up on cinder blocks and was constructed of logs that crossed at the corners. There was a wide covered deck right across the front with several benches and a swing facing the river. It was a pretty but rustic building that looked perfect in the surroundings.

Emily ran up the steps and flung open the door. "Wow! It's pretty big!" she hollered, running around inside. "There are even two bedrooms and a bathroom!"

"One bedroom is for us and Emily can use the other one while she's here," said his mother.

"Where do I sleep?" Henry asked. "In the bath tub?"

Emily laughed. "You're out of luck. There's no bath tub-just a shower. I guess you're on the floor!"

"Don't worry, Henry. There's a comfy pull-out sofa bed in the living room," shouted his mom.

Just great, he thought.

Henry looked around. He had to admit that he'd expected the cabin would be far more basic. This place was quite comfortable and even had a little kitchen. The rustic furniture included a table with four chairs, two sofas and a coffee table, beds and a few cabinets. But Henry suddenly realized there was no

TV.

"What? No TV?" Henry blurted out.

"There's no power right now, Henry. I'm sure you can do without TV for a few days," his father said. "Until then, we've got gas to cook with and flashlights for the nights."

"Oh," said Henry. "You mean we'll be pretty much in the dark?" The thought spooked him even more.

"Why don't you kids go and explore while it's still light," said his mom.

Emily grabbed Henry's sleeve and dragged him out to the deck before he could even open his mouth to object. He would have been happy to have stayed in the cabin.

"Let's be back here by dark, though, Em. Okay?" he said as she raced down the steps.

"No worries, I took a flashlight," she replied, waving it at him.

"Oh, okay," Henry drew in a deep breath. There was nothing more he could say. He didn't want to appear too chicken in front of a girl. He grabbed the can of mosquito repellant that his mom had placed strategically by the back door and sprayed it all over.

"Hey! Easy with that stuff!" Emily complained.

She coughed loudly, but Henry knew it was more for effect. "So, do you want to walk back and look at the cottage or shall we go down to the river?" he asked.

"The cottage for sure. I just want to meet Orlando! Do you think he's more likely to come out at dusk?"

"I hope not," said Henry. "Meeting him in daylight was bad enough."

They walked back to the main clearing and started to wade through the weeds towards the old cottage.

"This place is so cool!" Emily kept saying.

She clambered over the rubble like she was a professional mountain climber. Henry watched her easily navigate the nails and the planks of wood. He could hardly keep up. She hopped up the steps onto the rotten timbers of the old front porch and approached the door.

Henry watched in horror as she reached out for the knob. "Stop! Don't touch!" he hollered.

Emily turned toward him with a surprised look on her face. "What's wrong?"

"Let's go round the door-not through it," said Henry.

"Why? It looks so cool standing there on its own. It's like the door to nowhere!"

"It's pretty unstable. It might fall on us," was all Henry could think to say. He hadn't told her about his previous strange experience and wasn't ready to go though that a second time.

"Oh, okay." She climbed over the fallen walls and

onto the concrete pad.

Henry followed her. Together they stood facing the inside of the door. The paint was peeling off this side too, yet once again the shiny door knob looked new.

"So weird . . . it's just so weird," she giggled. "What is holding this door upright?"

Henry shrugged. He couldn't figure it out either.

They walked around the floor area trying to work out where the various rooms might have once been. The back wall of the house remained the most intact and some of the internal walls were still standing too. The kitchen sink and a few lower cupboards in the back corner of the house instantly identified where the kitchen used to be. There was a broken window above the kitchen sink and tattered curtains flapped in the breeze. On the countertop were some plates and bowls, as if someone had suddenly left the house after having a meal.

"Spooky," said Emily.

"This is more spooky," said Henry, pointing towards a toilet that was standing all on its own.

The light was fading. Henry felt a little nervous about making their way back over the rubble in the dark. "Hey, Em. I think we should go," he announced.

"We've got to call your ghost first, since he obviously isn't going to appear on his own."

"Maybe it's because you're here," Henry said

hopefully.

"Orlando . . . Orlando C. Phelps . . . we're calling you to appear," shouted Emily.

They waited a few seconds.

"Orlando Phelps, we want to talk to you!" she shouted again.

Nothing happened. Henry realized his heart was pounding. "Let's go, Em."

"Or-lan-do!" Emily almost sang his name.

They waited.

"Nah," said Henry. "He's not coming. Give it up, Em. It's nearly dark. We should go."

Emily sighed with disappointment. "Okay. Maybe he'll come tomorrow."

The door slammed behind them with a loud bang!

They turned instinctively.

There was a rush of cold air.

Henry shivered.

Emily shone the flashlight at the door.

"Ahhhh!" Henry screamed. He grabbed Emily's arm.

Standing with his back to the door was a man dressed in an ornate military uniform. Instantly Henry could see that the man had only one leg! His left leg was missing from above the knee. He had dark receding hair, heavy eyebrows and a mustache that curled upwards at the ends. His uniform was unlike anything Henry had seen before. The high-collared jacket was navy, with a double-breasted red front and gold brocade shoulder pads. He seemed weighed down with medals hung around his neck and pinned to his chest.

Henry remembered the ghost list he had made. The man's face was white and distorted and Henry was freezing cold. He was definitely seeing another apparition!

"Orlando?" questioned Emily. "Are you Orlando Phelps?"

Henry gulped. This was not Orlando. "No, Em," he whispered. "It's not. It's not him." But somehow the ghost in front of him looked familiar and he couldn't figure out why.

The ghost looked Henry right in the eye and, using a crutch, hobbled towards him. "Are you Orlando?" he asked in a deep voice with a hint of a foreign accent.

"M . . . me?" stammered Henry. "N . . . n . . . no, I'm not. I'm Henry."

"And I'm Emily," she added.

"I am looking for Orlando Phelps," the ghost replied.

"He's around here somewhere," said Emily, with not a hint of nervousness in her voice. "We're kind of looking for him too."

"If you see him, please tell him that I have been

searching for him."

"And who should we say is looking for him?" Emily ploughed on fearlessly.

"Tell him that El Presidente wants to talk to him."

"Okay, El Presidente," said Emily. "We'll pass on your message."

He placed his left arm across his stomach and bowed. "Muchas gracias, Emily, mi cosa dulce."

"Mi cosa dulce?" questioned Emily.

"My sweet thing," translated El Presidente.

The door banged again and in the second that Henry blinked, the ghost was gone.

Henry realized his legs were trembling while Emily seemed totally unfazed by the whole experience. "Well, that wasn't Orlando, for sure," he told her. "Orlando has both of his legs!"

"Wow!" said Emily excitedly. "I've just seen a ghost! I can't believe it!"

"Em, what I can't believe is that you're not at all freaked out!"

"You know I've always wanted to see one and I never thought I would. This is way cool! That was the best experience ever! Do you realize that we just communicated with a ghost! He even called me by my name. And he said that I was a sweet thing. I think I'll become one of those ghost hunters. Maybe I should start a blog or something . . ."

"Oh, good grief!" muttered Henry.

They clambered back over the rubble. It had now gone dark. Emily wasn't doing a very good job of directing the beam of the flashlight, and Henry couldn't see where he was walking. He stumbled and recovered several times, thankful that he hadn't sprained an ankle.

"Who do you think he was?" asked Emily when they reached the grass.

"No idea," said Henry. "Not sure I want to find out, either."

"Aww . . . come on, Henry. You've got to admit that El Presidente seemed really nice."

"Seemed," stressed Henry.

Emily groaned. "I told you that ghosts don't usually hurt you."

"Usually," reiterated Henry.

Emily ignored his comment and carried on excitedly. "So now you have two ghosts on the property. How cool is that?"

"Let's get out of here, before we have a third one," said Henry sarcastically. But deep down he was very serious. One ghost was bad enough, two ghosts were even more frightening and he didn't think he could cope if a third started popping up!

Emily plowed ahead with the flashlight, apparently caught up in the whole experience. Henry tried to keep up in the dark, wishing he was back in the cabin. It was a cloudy night so there was little light from the moon. Suddenly he walked straight into something hard.

"Owwww!" he yelled.

Emily turned and shone the beam in his direction. "Are you okay back there?"

Henry grabbed his big toe on his right foot and hopped around for a few seconds. He could also feel that he had grazed his thigh. What had he just walked into? Something white was sticking above the weeds.

"Em! Bring the flashlight-quick!"

"What have you found?"

"I don't know." Henry pulled back some of the grass. It looked like a huge white tombstone.

Emily shone the beam of light down towards the ground. She helped him tug at clumps of grass in an effort to clear the area around the stone.

"It's some kind of grave stone, I think," said Henry. "Wonder if one of our ghosts was buried here."

"No, it's not a grave," said Emily, shining the beam higher. "Look . . . it's a historical marker."

Near the top of the stone there was an engraving of a star surrounded by a wreath and underneath, some words.

"Read what it says," she ordered.

"Well, move closer and shine the light on the

words so that I can see them," said Henry.

Emily inched closer.

"Listen to this," said Henry. He began to read the words aloud.

SITE OF
"OROZIMBO"
HOME OF DR. JAMES A. E. PHELPS, A MEMBER OF THE "OLD THREE HUNDRED" OF AUSTIN'S COLONY, HOSPITAL SURGEON OF THE TEXAS ARMY AT SAN JACINTO. HERE SANTA ANNA WAS DETAINED AS A PRISONER FROM JULY TO NOVEMBER, 1836.

Henry gasped. Santa Anna? Could this be for real?

Emily was jumping up and down. "There! I told you! Our research was right. James Phelps owned Orozimbo, and so I'll bet it was his son, Orlando, that you saw."

Henry was silent. He was in shock. Orlando? Who cared about Orlando Phelps when Santa Anna, president of Mexico several times over, and the man who sent the Mexican army to the Alamo, had been held prisoner right where his parents were going to build their new home! This had to be his connection to Santa Anna that Charlie had talked about!

"Henry!" Emily shook him. "Say something!"

"Did you not read all of it?" he finally responded. "Santa Anna was right here! He was a prisoner at Orozimbo!" Now this was cool! It was something he could tell all his friends.

"Oh, okay," Emily remarked flatly. "So what?"

"So what?" Henry reiterated. "Don't you get it?" He looked at her in disbelief. El Presidente-our second ghost," he replied. "He's Santa Anna!"

Chapter 6

It poured with rain for most of Saturday and Henry was bored by early evening. Without electricity there was no TV and no computer, and now his cell phone had died. They had played board games for five hours solidly and he was all played out.

The others were engrossed in their books, though he guessed they wouldn't be for much longer. The light was fading fast and his mom only had a limited supply of batteries for their flashlights. His father was reading something political, his mother was buried in a mystery, and Emily had a thick fantasy book open across her lap.

Henry got up and walked into one of the bedrooms, yawning as he went. This was depressing weather. He kicked off his shoes and knelt on the bed, looking through the window, watching the rain gush off the roof in torrents. At least they weren't camping!

There was a loud clap of thunder followed immediately by a flash of lightning. The brightness lit up the almost-dark room. The storm was close. He listened to the familiar sounds of nature. He could hear branches cracking and falling to the ground with a thud all around the cabin. Hurricane Ike was still fresh in his memory even though he had only been seven years old at the time. He'd never forget the howling of the wind and the sounds of the straining trees during that powerful storm. This storm was tame in comparison!

But what did he hear in the distance? Was that the sound of howling dogs? He laughed. With weather like this there were all kinds of noises to be heard. He was probably imagining it.

But, no-there it was again! It was an ungodly baying sound-and quite loud this time. There were definitely dogs close by-and with that noise there had to be a whole pack of them! It sounded as if they were in distress in the stormy weather. Chills ran down his spine. Could it be a pack of coyotes? He knew that there were many that roamed in these parts.

He pressed his face to the window pane to try to see something outside. The rain running down the pane and the darkness made it difficult to see more than a few feet past the window. He stared into the black beyond, his breath on the glass making it even harder to see anything.

Suddenly, right in his face, appeared the snout of a snarling wild dog!

"Ahhhh!" Henry leaped back from the window in shock, falling off the bed in the process.

His heart was pounding as he looked up at the window from the floor. Now there were two dogs snarling at the window! Their enormous teeth were bared and their huge black noses were pressed to the glass. He could hear their growls above the noise of the storm-even with the glass and the thick timber walls in between.

They were unlike any dogs or coyotes he had seen before. Their unusual white color seemed to glow in the dark and they looked thin and emaciated as if they hadn't eaten in weeks. The viciousness in their dark glazed-looking eyes mesmerized him.

Now they were jumping and clawing at the window as if they were trying to get to him! Were it not for the glass, Henry knew he would have been in their jaws! Were they that hungry? He could hear the scraping of their claws on the glass. His heart beat faster. What if the glass should break?

A third dog suddenly appeared at the window, snarling and growling like the others. But this one was eerily pink in color. Henry shuddered. "Ewwww!" It looked as if someone had skinned the fur off its back!

"Get lost! Get out of here!" he screamed at them.

His mother, father and Emily came tearing into the room.

"What's happened?" they questioned in unison.

Henry was curled up on the floor, shaking. He could hardly get out the words. "Wild dogs . . . at the window! Look! Look!"

They all turned towards the window. "Where, Henry?" his mother asked. "I don't see anything!" She stood at the end of the bed and leaned closer to the glass to look. "There's nothing out there, Henry."

Henry stared at the window in disbelief. The dogs had vanished! Perhaps they saw everyone come into the bedroom and ran away? He listened for their howls, but all he could hear was the wind and the torrential rain.

His father helped him up off the floor. "Are you sure you didn't fall asleep and dream it?"

Henry was still trembling. He sat on the bed with his back under the window. "I swear! There were three of them snarling at me!"

"Probably coyotes," said his mom. "You're fine, anyway, and that's the important thing."

"It was probably the branches moving in the storm, casting shadows across the window and scraping on the roof," said his father. Henry knew he was trying to give a more scientific explanation. "Coyotes wouldn't come that close to the cabin."

Henry shook his head. "I know what I saw."

"Okay, if you say so," said his mother in an appeasing tone. "But I don't know how you could see much from the floor, anyway."

With that, his father patted him on the shoulder and his parents left the room.

Emily sat on the bed next to him. "I know a little bit about coyotes from a project I did in school. I didn't want to contradict your father, but they will come close to a house if they are hungry enough. I read about one case where a coyote jumped up at someone's kitchen window. So I think it's possible that you saw some. "

Henry knelt on the bed, rested his elbows on the windowsill, and stared out the window. The lightning flashed brightly again, shining on the glass. "Yes!" he shrieked. "I knew I hadn't dreamed it!"

"What do you see?" asked Emily, kneeling next to him.

"Look closely, Em!"

When the next flash of lightning lit up the glass she turned and smiled broadly at him. "Those sure look like muddy paw prints to me."

"Yeah, and you can see the long streaks of mud where they clawed at the window."

"I knew you were telling the truth. Shall I get your parents to see before the rain washes them away?"

"Nah. I didn't tell Mom and Dad everything," he whispered.

Emily leaned closer to him. "What? Tell me!" she demanded.

"Promise you won't laugh?"

"Pinkie swear," she said, pointing her little finger at him.

"Nah, that's a girl thing," said Henry.

"Well, go on, tell me the rest!"

"I don't really think they could have been coyotes," said Henry.

"Why not?"

"Two of the dogs were a translucent white and they glowed in the dark! The third one was bright pink and it looked like it only had skin and no fur! It was like seeing something out of a horror video game!"

Emily didn't laugh, for which Henry was thankful. She just stared at him, her mouth gaping. "Wow!" she finally said. "That's soooooo cool!"

Henry rolled his eyes. Cool? "You believe me, Em, don't you?"

"Of course, I do! After what we saw yesterday, I'll believe almost anything!"

"Thanks, Em. I'm so glad you came."

"So am I. I've never had so much fun in all of my

life."

"Fun? What, here at Orozimbo?" questioned Henry. "How can you say that this is fun . . . or cool? I hate it here!"

Secretly he had to admit that he had never had an adventure like this one before-and it was kind of exciting. But every bone in his body was telling him that this was just the beginning!

Chapter 7

Henry was ecstatic to be going home and wasn't sure he wanted to return to Orozimbo . . . ever! He hadn't slept all night, listening for the sound of wild dogs. He'd felt very vulnerable lying on the sofa and not tucked up in bed. The events of the last week had certainly taken their toll. Now he felt as though he needed a vacation from the vacation!

The ground was a boggy mess after the torrential rain of the night before. His parents had decided they should go home for a while and wait for everything to dry up. Henry helped to load up the car, traipsing up and down the path through the thick mud. His trainers were caked in it. But he didn't care. The sooner they got in the car and drove through those gates, the happier he would be.

Emily gloomily dragged her bag down the steps. She looked really sad to be leaving-but at least his parents had said she could come back with them later in the week.

Occasionally Henry dozed off in the back of the car, dreaming about dogs and ghosts. As they approached the center of Angleton he could see the sign to the Historical Museum. He seemed to get a strange tingling sensation in his legs as they passed by the sign. He needed to find out more about the history of Orozimbo Plantation and particularly about its connection to Santa Anna. Was he really thinking that? He'd always thought he hated history, yet he was actually contemplating walking to the historical museum!

Charlie had been right. Henry knew he had found that connection to history and now he felt compelled to dig deeper and deeper. Perhaps that would help him rest easy and enjoy Orozimbo rather than be terrified about going there.

They pulled up to Emily's house. His father opened the trunk of the Explorer, and Henry got out of the car to help her with her bag. "Em," he whispered. "Wanna walk into town with me tomorrow morning?"

"Sure," she said, putting on her backpack. "What are we buying?"

"We're not buying anything. I'll explain tomorrow."

She gave him a quizzical look. "Okay. I'll see you around 10 a.m.. Text me when you're leaving your house."

* * * * * *

It was a sweltering Monday morning and the walk into town was a killer. Emily was excited when Henry divulged that their reason for going was to find out about the history of Orozimbo.

They arrived at the huge Brazoria County Historical Museum on East Cedar Street. An impressive large, gray stucco building with a cream-colored stone trim and lots of long rectangular windows, the museum dominated the smaller buildings on the surrounding streets.

Henry led the way up the stone steps and into the high-ceilinged entrance hall. They approached the information desk and asked where they should go to find out about Orozimbo. Their voices echoed in the vast space.

The lady staffing the desk directed them up to the second floor and told them to look for Michael or Jamie. For once it was Emily who lagged behind as they climbed up the iron steps. Henry was on a mission and he couldn't rest until he had the information he wanted. Finally they reached an office door that read 'Curator,' and they stepped inside.

Henry scanned the room. There was a wealth of books and documents piled high on shelves and tables and he assumed the filing cabinets and large chests of drawers also contained historical information. They were definitely in the right place!

A gentleman was working at a computer desk directly in front of them. He was a large man, smartly dressed, with long hair tied back in a braid. He looked up and seemed surprised to see two children standing in the doorway.

"Hello, there!" he said with a big wide smile. "I'm Michael Bailey and this is my assistant, Jamie Murray. How can we help you youngsters?"

Jamie was an older lady with gray hair and black-rimmed glasses. Henry thought her warm smile was very welcoming and reassuring for someone who didn't like history!

"Um . . . my name is Henry and this is my cousin, Emily."

"Well, don't stand in the doorway, kids! Come on in, and let's see if we can answer your questions," said Jamie.

"Well . . . I don't know if you have any information about a place called Orozimbo Plantation," began Henry. "Emily and I have seen some weird stuff there in the last few days and we're wondering about its history."

Michael seemed to come alive. He almost leaped off his chair in excitement. "How much time do you have?" he laughed."I could talk for days about the place."

"Really?" said Henry.

"Michael could talk for days about anything historical," said Jamie with a broad grin, "but Orozimbo is one of his favorite subjects. Come into this room, kids, and I'll pull out everything that we have."

They stepped through the archway into another equally crowded room. There was a large table in the center piled high with charts and papers, a computer against one wall, and cabinets and shelves stacked full of information. Henry was dazed. He wondered how Michael and Jamie could ever find anything.

Jamie went straight to a filing cabinet by the door. "Let's see . . . Orozimbo Plantation, Columbia, Texas." She pulled out two overflowing manila folders and placed them in the center of the huge wooden table. "Take a seat, kids, and I'll show you documents and tons of information that would take you hours to find on the internet."

Henry couldn't believe the amount of old newspaper clippings and original photos that came out of the folder.

"So what do you want to know first?" Michael

asked.

Henry didn't know where to start. "My parents have just bought 43 acres of the old Orozimbo Plantation," he began.

"You're so lucky," said Michael. "You'll love living there!"

Henry gulped. Lucky? Dare he tell them how he really felt?

"Actually, he hates it!" Emily chimed in for him.

Michael looked stunned. "Really?"

"Well, I'm sure we can change your mind," said Jamie. "It's really an amazing place."

"We've both seen some very weird stuff up there in the last few days," said Emily.

"Yeah, it's freaked me out!" Henry admitted. "My parents are about to build a house and I swear the place is haunted."

Jamie and Michael exchanged glances. They were both silent. Henry wasn't sure that he liked Jamie's expression and he had a bad feeling about what was coming next.

"Orozimbo is supposed to be haunted," said Jamie. "But no one has ever been able to identify the ghosts or has any proof that the ghosts exist. Most people believe that the sightings are just stories passed down to scare intruders off the property."

"Or stories that are told in Brazoria County to

boost tourism," added Michael.

"Do you believe in ghosts?" Henry asked them.

"Definitely!" said Jamie quickly. "We had a young man here about a year ago who saw the ghost of Cabeza de Vaca! I was skeptical to begin with, but we tied a lot of the information he gave us and the things he had seen directly to the history of San Luis Pass."

"So now she's a believer," added Michael. "Me? I'm not so sure . . ."

"So why don't you tell us what you have seen," interrupted Jamie, "and we'll see if we can fill in the wonderful history."

Henry drew in a deep breath. "Well, we know that Orozimbo was an old cotton plantation owned by the Phelps family. We found out a bit about Dr. James Phelps on the internet. I was walking around the ruins of the cottage and I think I saw Orlando Phelps."

"But he was mean!" added Emily. "He pointed a gun at Henry and told him to get off his property or he would regret it!"

Jamie and Michael were both wide-eyed.

"I actually saw him twice," Henry continued. "He was quite young-about 18 or 19. He was dressed like someone who had fought at the Alamo-you know, with a fringed jacket and wide-brimmed hat. He had a rifle and said he would defend Orozimbo just like he had defended Texas from the raiding Mexicans."

"Hmmm," said Michael. "Well, what you are describing certainly does seem to fit Orlando and what we know of him."

"He somehow managed to take me back in time and show me what the old plantation home used to look like. It had this enormous entrance hall and a sweeping staircase up to the second floor."

"Like in this drawing?" Jamie asked. She placed a picture in front of him.

"Just like that!" shrieked Henry. He pointed to the picture. "There's the old grandfather clock that I saw!"

"Fascinating!" said Michael. "Well, let me tell you a few stories about Orlando's life and let's see if anything ties in with what you saw."

Jamie fetched some bottles of water and handed them around.

Michael pulled up another chair and started the tale. "Orlando grew up on the plantation, although he did go to school in Mississippi for a few years. He signed up for what was known as the Mier Expedition in 1842. He was only 20 years old at the time. The Mexicans had continued attacking over the border after the peace treaties had been signed at Velasco."

Henry turned to Emily and said, "Velasco was the first capital of Texas and it's called Surfside Beach today,"

Jamie smiled. "I can tell you've seen the big

stone!"

Emily looked confused.

"I'll tell you about it later," said Henry.

"So General Sam Houston sent an armed force in an effort to avenge the Mexican attacks," Michael continued. "However, he changed his orders at the last minute and called his men back. But several hundred men, including Orlando, decided to carry on. They marched over the border and attacked a Mexican stronghold at Mier. It went very badly and they were captured and sentenced to be executed."

"So Orlando died?" Henry cut in. "Is that why I'm seeing his ghost at Orozimbo?"

"No, he didn't die. He was very lucky. The men who were captured were told that one in every ten of the prisoners would be executed. They were given a jar of white beans with some black beans amongst them. Then they were all blindfolded and told to take a bean from the jar. If you drew a black bean you would die and if you drew a white bean you would be saved."

"So Orlando drew a white bean and was saved," said Emily.

Jamie smiled. "No, he didn't! He actually drew a black bean!"

"Huh?" said Emily. "So what happened?"

"How was he saved?" asked Henry.

"The list of the men to be executed was given to Santa Anna." Michael showed them a photograph of the Mexican president.

Henry's stomach jumped. He felt wild with excitement when he saw the picture. "Santa Anna was definitely the second ghost that I saw!" he blurted out. "That's exactly how he looked, with all those medals round his neck. Emily saw him too!"

Emily nodded. "That's the ghost we saw, for sure. He was looking for Orlando!"

Michael and Jamie had gaping mouths and wide eyes so Henry knew that he really had their attention.

"I'm sure that you both know he is probably the most hated man in Texas history," said Michael.

"Yes, I think he led the Mexicans at the Battle of the Alamo and he had over 300 prisoners killed at Goliad. Then he was captured at the Battle of San Jacinto, right?" questioned Henry.

"Wow, Henry!" said Emily. "For someone who doesn't like history, you know a lot more than I do!"

"I just have a good memory. I learned all that in Texas history class." And some from Charlie too, he thought.

"You are correct on all counts," said Michael. "But most people don't know that Santa Anna, even though he was known as a man without integrity, did actually have a good side and showed some compassion at times. He was not all bad."

"He was nice to me," said Emily. "Not scary at all."

"So what did Santa Anna do that was good?" asked Henry, eager to hear since Charlie had refused to tell him many details.

"Well, Dr. James Phelps, Orlando's father, had been kind to Santa Anna when he was a prisoner at Orozimbo from July to November 1836."

"That's another fascinating story, which we'll have to save for another time," Jamie quickly cut in.

Michael nodded and continued. "When Santa Anna saw the name Orlando Phelps on the list for execution he called for the young man to be brought to him. Orlando confirmed that his father was Dr. James Phelps. So, Santa Anna, in gratitude for what Dr. Phelps did for him while he was a prisoner, saved Orlando's life."

"But there's more," said Jamie. "Santa Anna gave Orlando some fine clothing, a gift for his mother and also $500 in gold! He sent him with an escort to the border to make sure that the young man got safely home to Orozimbo."

"So they were actually friends?" asked Henry.

"I wouldn't go that far," said Michael. "But Santa Anna certainly is responsible for saving Orlando's life."

"So why would Orlando be trying to frighten me away from Orozimbo? And why would Santa Anna be looking for Orlando?"

"I have no idea. I think you will have to work that out for yourselves," he said with a smile. "That's a great summer vacation ghost mystery for both of you to solve."

"Perhaps Orlando buried the gold at Orozimbo and Santa Anna wants it back!" said Emily excitedly. "It would be worth a fortune today!"

"Could be," said Jamie. "A lot of ghost stories seem to involve buried treasure, and the boy who saw the ghost of Cabeza de Vaca last year did actually find buried gold!"

Henry thought Emily was about to fall off the chair in her excitement.

"He did? Wow! Then I'll bet that's what this whole thing is about!" she shrieked. "Orlando is protecting his gold and Santa Anna is looking for it because he wants it back! What if we find it first? How cool would that be?"

Henry was horrorstruck. "You've got to be kidding, Em! No way are we looking for the gold! The last thing I want to do is upset these ghosts so that they haunt me even more!"

"There are many other reasons why ghosts appear," said Jamie. "It's usually because they have a connection with a person or a place."

There it was again, thought Henry-that word

connection.

"But Orozimbo and Henry are the connection," said Emily. His family is about to move to Orozimbo and might find the gold. That's why Orlando and Santa Anna want Henry and his family gone from Orozimbo! Don't you see? It makes perfect sense!"

Henry sighed. It was not a theory he liked! If he and Emily found the gold the ghosts could haunt him forever. And if the gold stayed buried at Orozimbo, then Orlando would always be there to protect it and Santa Anna would always be there looking for it. Oh, boy! He wouldn't be rid of them either way! Now he felt as though he needed to do a whole lot more research about Orozimbo and its owners.

"Why don't you copy some of these newspaper articles and take them home to read," said Jamie, as if she could read his mind. "You never know . . . there might be information that supports your theory or other clues might be buried somewhere on one of the pages." She sorted out some of the relevant clippings and ran off copies for each of them. "There you go, kids-happy reading!"

"Of course, there's a lot of information to be found on the internet too," added Michael.

"Well, thank you, sir and ma'am, for your help," said Henry. "It's been very interesting."

"I'll say," said Emily. "Thanks a bunch!"

"Let us know if you come to any conclusions," shouted Jamie as they left.

They walked down the curved metal staircase, carrying the folder. Henry was surprised at how interesting the morning had been, and he knew he still wanted to dig deeper, just as Charlie had predicted.

"You didn't ask them about the dogs that you saw," said Emily.

Henry shrugged. "It was terrifying at the time, but I don't think that wild dogs trying to get out of the storm have anything to do with Orlando Phelps or Santa Anna."

"Maybe," said Emily. "But you have to admit . . . it's one more weird thing that has happened at Orozimbo."

Chapter 8

"I don't suppose you want to go to Surfside Beach, do you?" asked Henry's mom as he walked in the door. "The builder is going to mark the footings for the house later in the week so I need to meet with the architect at Mrs. Zachariah's beach house."

"Sure!" said Henry enthusiastically. For once, he didn't mind going with her since he was eager to talk to Charlie. He had a feeling that the old man might be able to tell him a whole lot more about Santa Anna.

They pulled up under Mrs. Zachariah's house to keep the car out of the hot Texas sun.

"Is it okay if I go to the Surfside Beach museum?" Henry asked.

"Fine, but keep your cell on in case I'm ready to leave before you're back," replied his mother, as she climbed the steps to the beach house.

Henry walked along the hot asphalt road, hoping that Charlie would be volunteering today. Just as he began to climb the steps to the museum entrance, Charlie was coming out. Henry had timed it perfectly.

"Hey, young man!" Charlie waved at him.

"Hi, Charlie!"

"It's good to see you again! What brings you back to our little museum? I thought you didn't like history," he said with a cheeky grin.

Henry smiled at him. "I found that connection you were talking about."

"Oh, you did, eh? Come up here and sit in the shade with me. I want to hear all about it."

Henry ran up the steps and sat down on the narrow wooden bench under the overhang of the roof, where it was much cooler. "I was kind of hoping you would have some time to tell me more stuff about Santa Anna."

"Sure! What do you want to know?" Charlie stretched out his legs. "I've got as much time as you need today."

"Have you ever heard of Orozimbo?"

Charlie's eyes lit up. "Ah! But of course! It's the grand old plantation out in Columbia where Santa Anna was held prisoner for five months after he was captured. So you found out about that, did you?"

"We now own part of it," said Henry. "That's my connection. My parents are building a house there."

Charlie raised his eyebrows and stared at him. "Well, I wasn't expecting you to say that!"

You'll not be expecting this either, thought Henry. "When we were there at the weekend, I saw the ghost of Santa Anna! My cousin was with me and she saw him too!"

"You don't say!" replied Charlie. Henry couldn't tell from his expression if the old man believed him or not.

"He said he was looking for Orlando Phelps and that if we saw Orlando we were to tell him that El Presidente was looking for him."

"Gee! You have had quite an exciting few days since I saw you last!" said Charlie.

"Yeah, I saw the ghost of Orlando too. He really scared me. He pointed a rifle at me and told me to get off his property or I would regret it!"

"Did he, now?"

Henry thought Charlie seemed completely dazed, as if he didn't really know what to say in response, but he certainly didn't question the ghostly sightings so Henry plowed on. "I'm scared to go back to Orozimbo right now. I'm trying to work out why the ghosts keep appearing so that maybe I can get them to leave. I even went to the Historical Museum in Angleton-"

"Oh, you did, did you?" Charlie chuckled and then

slapped him on the back. "Good for you!"

"So I know how Santa Anna saved Orlando and gave him $500 in gold. My cousin, Emily, thinks that Santa Anna wants his gold back and that we should look for it too."

Charlie laughed loudly. "No, I don't think that's the case. Tell your cousin not to start digging up every inch of Orozimbo anytime soon! I doubt she'll find anything."

"Why not?" asked Henry.

"Santa Anna was a wealthy man, and $500 was nothing to him. He gave the money as a gift to Orlando, and although he could be very cruel-even against his own people-he would have honored that gift. Besides, I should think that Orlando's family spent the money a long time ago."

"Oh," said Henry. "So, if gold is not the reason the ghosts are there, what is?"

Charlie raked his fingers through his beard and leaned back against the wall. "Well, I don't know much about ghosts. I do believe they exist and I have certainly had many people recount sightings of ghosts to me over the years. So all I can do is tell you some more stories about Orozimbo and you will have to piece everything together yourself."

"Can you tell me why Santa Anna saved Orlando?"

The Ghosts of Orozimbo

"Santa Anna was first held prisoner at another plantation in Columbia owned by Major Patton. It wasn't far from Orozimbo. While he was there, Santa Anna managed to get hold of some poisoned wine. He wanted to die because he thought that he would be shot as a prisoner. Major Patton found him writhing on the ground, immediately picked him up and placed him in the family carriage. Then he drove him as fast as he could to see Dr. James Phelps, who pumped Santa Anna's stomach and saved his life."

"Wow! So he stayed with the Phelps family after that?" asked Henry.

"Correct. Santa Anna was a prisoner at Orozimbo for five months. The Phelps family treated him very well. They allowed him to sleep on the finest feather bed and they gave him the best food that they could offer. It is also said that there was an occasion when Mrs. Phelps saved his life by throwing her arms around Santa Anna to prevent a soldier from shooting him!"

"So they must have liked him," said Henry.

"I think so, but mostly I just think that the Phelpses were good people. As I said, we only hear the bad things about Santa Anna, but there are a few stories that show he had a good side. He was certainly appreciative of how he was treated by the Phelps family. In return he managed to get back a prized family Bible that had been taken from the Orozimbo Plantation by Mexican soldiers. He also sent presents of fine blankets to Mrs. Phelps every Christmas and, as you know, six years later he saved their son, Orlando, when he was captured in Mexico."

"I guess he owed them one," said Henry.

Charlie laughed again. "You certainly could say that-one or two, or even three!"

"Thanks, Charlie. That was an interesting story."

"Hope it helps."

Henry sighed. "It has helped me to understand the history of Orozimbo, but I'm still not looking forward to going back there tomorrow. I hope I don't see any more ghosts or vicious dogs."

"Vicious dogs?" questioned Charlie.

"Yeah, three of the ugliest looking wild dogs tried to get into our cabin during the storm on Saturday night. They were making this awful noise, clawing at the window and baring their teeth at me. It was very scary. But no one else saw them so I don't think my parents believe me. My mom thinks I could have seen coyotes, but I know they weren't. They looked nothing like coyotes. They looked more like starved wolves."

Charlie looked suddenly pasty. "Were two of them glowing white and the other one pink with no fur?"

Henry could feel his jaw drop. He gulped. "How did you know that?"

"Because, young man, you saw the Hounds of Orozimbo!"

"What are the Hounds of Orozimbo?"

"Ghost dogs, Henry . . . they're ghost dogs."

Henry stared at him. "Ghost dogs?" He gulped. "Are you telling me those dogs weren't alive-that they were ghosts too?"

"It's another story that is told about Orozimbo," said Charlie. "A few people say they have actually seen the dogs but many, many people have heard their sorrowful baying."

"Oh, good grief!" said Henry. "Now I've got vicious ghost dogs and the ghost of Orlando Phelps trying to scare me away from Orozimbo!"

Chapter 9

Henry sat in the back of the car feeling completely and utterly sick on Tuesday morning. He hadn't slept properly in several days and now that the ground had dried, his parents couldn't be dissuaded from going straight back to Orozimbo. In fact, his mother had gotten quite cross with him and yelled at him to get in the car. He decided that he would just sit inside the cabin for the next few weeks!

At least the builders would be up there tomorrow and Emily was coming the day after, so he only had to survive two days on his own. Well, he wasn't really on his own with his parents there. But it felt like it.

They pulled through the gate and drove up to the clearing to unload the Explorer. The trail to the cabin had dried up so much after the hot weather of the last two days that already cracks were appearing in the mud.

Henry lugged his heavy backpack into the cabin. It contained the important folder of newspaper clippings from the museum, and it was heavy. His parents immediately spread the house plans out on the kitchen table and sat down to discuss them, so he went quietly into the second bedroom. At least he could sleep comfortably on a bed for a couple of nights before Emily returned and he was relegated back to sleeping on the sofa bed in the living room.

Henry sat on the bed and pulled the thick folder from his backpack. There was enough reading material to last him the next two days! Several articles covered Orlando Phelps and the Meir Expedition and many others were about Santa Anna being held prisoner at Orozimbo. He skipped those for now and continued looking through the pile, reading the headlines until he came across one titled, "The Hounds of Orozimbo." This he had to read! Unlike some of the other articles, which had clearly come from old newspapers, Henry saw that this one was a printout from a website called 'Fairweather Lewis.' Henry lay back on the bed and began to read.

"It was a moonless night with rain falling heavily when the rescue of Santa Anna was planned by

Mexican loyalists. Someone had given the guards and other members of the Phelps household drugged wine and everyone was sound asleep. All at once there was a terrible sound of baying, like a pack of hounds that had spotted their prey. One of the servants at Orozimbo awoke and swore that there were only three dogs-two white ones that glowed even on the moonless night and one that was pink and looked as though it had been skinned. All of them had strange glazed eyes and were half-starved. The servant raised the alarm and the dogs vanished."

Henry put the paper down for a minute. He swallowed hard. He wasn't sure if he felt more scared or reassured knowing that he hadn't imagined the whole incident. His hands shook as he continued reading . . .

"Santa Anna's rescuers fled in terror. No one knew where the dogs had come from. Dr. Phelps never owned any dogs and there were no dogs ever at Orozimbo. The hounds are still seen and heard on the plantation particularly on moonless rainy nights."

"Oh, boy," Henry muttered. "The dogs really are here at Orozimbo and that's exactly the weather we were having on Saturday night!"

His heart was thumping loudly as he read the final paragraph.

"Years later a man visited Orozimbo and was told the story of Santa Anna's attempted escape. He instantly recognized the dogs from the description. They had belonged to a man who lived in Washington-on-the Brazos, a long way away. He had gone to fight for Texas Independence and had to leave his dogs behind. The hounds seemed to know that their master wouldn't return. They had refused to eat and eventually disappeared.

The visitor to Orozimbo was surprised that the hounds could have traveled so far from their home. But then he added that their master was one of the 309 men murdered at Goliad by Santa Anna."

"Wow! Wow!" shrieked Henry. He leaped off the bed, clutching the paper, hardly able to contain himself. "Maybe the hounds weren't after me at all-they were still after Santa Anna! Perhaps they were warning me, to try and protect me from Santa Anna!"

Henry calmed himself and sat back down. Of course the whole story was pretty incredible to begin with, and it took a wild stretch of the imagination to think that the ghost dogs were still here at Orozimbo chasing Santa Anna more than 150 years later. And why would the dogs want to protect Henry, a boy from Angleton, from El Presidente? But he felt better inside believing that.

Henry closed the folder and took out his cell

phone. "Only one bar," he groaned. But it was enough to text Emily. 'Read story about Hounds of Orozimbo. What do u think? Tell me when u c me."

His phone buzzed.

'K,' she responded.

Henry went into the main room. His parents were still poring over the plans, arguing about where to put closets and certain interior doors. He walked onto the front porch and sat on the step. At least the storm had cleared the muggy air and there was a fresh cool breeze, which kept away the mosquitoes. But it was only 11 a.m. and he knew that in a couple of hours the temperatures would be back in the nineties and he would be sweating buckets. Henry could see part of the dilapidated cottage through the trees. There was something about it that fascinated him and it seemed to be calling him back. Now was the time to take a walk if he was going to.

Walk? What was he thinking? Wasn't he going to stay safely in the cottage until Emily arrived? The Hounds of Orozimbo might be chasing Santa Anna, but Orlando Phelps was still a threat! After all, Orlando carried a rifle and had gotten pretty angry at him . . . twice.

Henry tried to resist the urge to get off the step, but he couldn't. Before he knew it he was walking down the trail towards the pile of rubble. Perhaps it was curiosity . . . perhaps it was foolhardiness . . . or perhaps the ghosts were calling to him. But there seemed to be no turning back.

Henry passed the white historical marker that they had uncovered at the weekend and this time climbed more nimbly over the rubble. He stepped up on to the old front porch and approached the door. He wondered if it made a difference how he entered the building. If he went through the door would he see Orlando again? If he went around the door would he see Santa Anna again? After all he had learned about both men in the last couple of days, he wasn't sure he wanted to meet either of them. However, deep down inside he knew he would never sleep peacefully at Orozimbo if he didn't.

Henry put his hand on the doorknob and turned slowly. The door swung open with little effort. Henry stepped forward, inching over the threshold, not knowing what to expect. He stood on the concrete slab on the other side of the door.

Bang! The door slammed closed behind him. Had that been the breeze?

A cold chill swept over him. His head felt suddenly light. His vision blurred as it had before. He staggered a few steps. Even though it was distinctly chilly in the room, he was sweating madly. He felt someone's presence beside him. He was scared, but this time he didn't yell out. He waited . . .

When his vision cleared, Orlando Phelps, still dressed in the militia clothing, stood directly in front of him, rifle in hand. Although the gun was not pointed directly at Henry, Orlando's demeanor was definitely aggressive.

Orlando glared at Henry with piercing eyes, frowning so intently that his eyebrows seemed to meet in the middle. "I thought I told you not to return!" Orlando screamed. "You are trespassing once again on my property! Do I have to hold you as my prisoner?"

Henry gulped. "Ummm . . . no . . . no, you don't. I am not a Mexican soldier that you have to fight. This is my property too! I am also trying to protect it!"

Orlando's face reddened. "Orozimbo belongs to my family! It always will! I will protect it for all time-not you!"

"I am Texan too. I know you are Orlando Phelps and I know all about you and your family and how you owned Orozimbo. I know how you were the Captain of the Alamo Guard and I know that you went on the Mier Expedition in 1842 . . ."

"Then if you know all of that, how can you stake a claim to my land?"

"Well, I'm not trying to steal your gold, if that's what you think," added Henry, just to see what

97

Orlando's response would be.

"Gold? What gold?"

"The $500 that Santa Anna gave to you in 1843."

Orlando roared with laughter. "There's no gold! That money was brought back from Mexico and given to my family. It was used to maintain this plantation. This land, and the house that was on it, has been in the Phelps family for years and I am protecting it for that reason-and not because of any gold on the property! I will protect it from you and I will protect it from Mexican raiders."

"But it doesn't belong to your family anymore! My name is Henry Garrison and my family, the Garrison family, owns this land legally."

Orlando's facial expression changed from anger to confusion. "Henry Garrison, did you say? That is an honorable name. It seems that you and I have a connection that I didn't know of," he responded.

Orlando's aggressive demeanor disappeared and he seemed to relax. Henry watched in amazement as the rifle once again flew from Orlando's hand and landed on the floor several feet away.

"Connection? What connection?" asked Henry. There was that word again!

"My past and your future are entwined. You must help me save the house."

"But the house is gone," said Henry. "It can't be

98

saved."

His words seemed to fall on deaf ears.

"Come with me and I will show you the lovely Orozimbo!" said Orlando.

Henry looked around and once again he was standing in the beautiful entrance hall at the foot of the enormous sweeping staircase.

This time Orlando led him up the stairs, then paused at the top and looked down into the grand hall below. "My parents acquired the land for this house in 1824 when I wasn't even two years old. They named it after an Indian chief. It is now a flourishing cotton plantation. We have many servants and slaves who work for us."

He continued along the landing and opened the door to one of the bedrooms. "Come in," he said, beckoning Henry to follow.

It was a large square room, decorated with family pictures. There was a beautiful dark wooden chest of drawers against one wall and a rocking chair in the corner. Between two large sash windows stood an enormous four-poster bed.

"Isn't the bedspread fine?" Orlando asked.

Henry ran his hands over the beautiful quilted fabric and nodded. "It's really nice."

"Santa Anna gave the bedspread to my mother as a gift," he said proudly. "You will see them in the other bedrooms too. He sent bedspreads to us every Christmas."

"So he was your friend, then?" asked Henry.

"Friend? He is no friend! He is the enemy!" said Orlando, suddenly changing his tone.

Henry thought it funny that Orlando talked of Santa Anna as if he were still alive, when Henry knew that El Presidente had died back in 1876. Of course, Orlando was also dead.

Orlando continued in a raised voice. "Santa Anna was responsible for the death of so many of my fellow Texans at Mier. Many of them were my close friends and for that I will never forgive him! He is a cruel man."

"But he saved your life, didn't he?" Henry questioned.

"I admit, he treated my family well and I owe him my life. But the battle for Texas must continue!"

Henry wondered if he dare deliver Santa Anna's message. He sucked in a deep breath and said, "Actually, Santa Anna is here at Orozimbo."

Orlando stared at him, his mouth agape. His rifle suddenly flew through the bedroom door and landed smack in his hands. "What do you mean he is here?" he asked, taking a defensive position at the door.

"I saw him yesterday. He wants to speak to you."

"What about?" snapped Orlando.

Henry shook his head. "I don't know."

The Ghosts of Orozimbo

"The man continues to send troops and organize raids over our borders even though he has signed official peace treaties. Is he finally going to accept our Texas independence, eleven years after The Battle of San Jacinto?" asked Orlando, peering round the door.

Henry was stunned. Eleven years after San Jacinto? Orlando thought he was still in 1847! "Ummmm . . . he didn't say," replied Henry, not knowing how else he could answer.

"Then I must gather my men! You, Henry Garrison, are my family. You are one of us. You must join us in this fight to save Orozimbo!"

"But Santa Anna wasn't armed!" called Henry as Orlando flew down the stairs, rifle in hand. "I don't think he was here to fight you!" Henry leaned over the railings at the top of the stairs and shouted, "He seemed quite friendly, really." But Orlando was already through the door.

Henry felt sick. How could things change so quickly? One minute Orlando thought Henry was the enemy and now he was family! How strange was that? Santa Anna was obviously a much bigger threat. Henry hoped that he hadn't just caused another battle between the Texans and the Mexicans!

It was definitely time to head back to the cabin. Henry made his way back down the staircase. But with each step it felt as though he couldn't quite put his foot all the way down on the step, until eventually it seemed as if he were treading on thin air. He grabbed onto the polished handrail for support.

As he reached the bottom of the stairs he noticed that the grandfather clock was gone and so was the beautiful woven carpet. As if by magic, the room had been transformed back to the present day. Now, all he could see were crumbling walls and the peeling varnish on the front door, which still stood unsupported in front of him.

Henry opened the door and stepped into the fresh summer breeze. It was only then that he realized he was shaking violently.

Chapter 10

"Henry! Get up!" his mother yelled. "It's nearly noon!"

"In a minute," he groaned.

Henry rolled over and stretched. He had stayed up very late engrossed in the newspaper clippings. It was as though he had an insatiable appetite for historical facts about Orozimbo. Of course, his brain had been so wired after all the reading that when he finally put his head on the pillow, he hadn't been able to sleep.

He had dreamed that he was marching beside Orlando Phelps to defend Orozimbo. He'd been wearing a suede jacket with long fringe on the shoulders and a dark brown hat with a wide brim, just like Orlando and the rest of his men. Behind Henry was the beautiful plantation house, constructed mainly of wood, standing proudly two stories high. The servants cheered them on as they approached the gate and a drummer beat a steady rhythm. Henry had his rifle at the ready . . . Santa Anna waited on the other side of the gate with his men . . .

"Henry! Get up now!" his mother yelled again.

"What is there to get up for?" Henry mumbled and rolled over.

"Henry!" This time his mother shook him. "The bulldozers are here! I thought you would want to watch them tear down the cottage and clear the rubble, especially as you obviously don't like it!"

"No!" shrieked Henry, sitting bolt upright. "They can't do that yet!"

He leaped out of bed, knocking the lamp off the bedside table. Something he'd read at midnight suddenly made sense!

His mother looked completely dumbfounded. "Why not?"

"Ummmm . . . because . . . there's stuff we need to save!"

He grabbed his shorts off the chair and, hopping from one leg to the other, put them on as he ran down the steps.

"Henry! Wait! What do we need to save?" shouted his mother after him.

The Ghosts of Orozimbo

Henry tore down the path to the clearing. The noise was deafening. How could he have slept through this? A huge orange bulldozer was being backed off an even larger trailer. An excavator was already in position on the site, with its engine revving.

The excavator moved closer to the remaining walls of the cottage. Henry watched as its tracks easily climbed the mound of debris. It was like watching a tank in a war movie climbing over ruined buildings, crushing everything in its path. Oh, no! He didn't want everything crushed!

"No! Wait!" screamed Henry. "I want to save some of the wood! And I want to save the door!" If the door were destroyed would he ever see Orlando Phelps and the old Orozimbo again? There had to be something he could do!

He kept shouting but it was impossible to shout over the noise of the machinery.

Henry stood helplessly as the huge machines moved in to demolish the cottage. Suddenly he felt overcome by sadness. Tears crept into the corners of his eyes. He brushed them away. Only now did he completely understand the value of what was in front of him. There was irreplaceable history in that pile of rubble, and soon it would all be gone forever.

Unless . . .

Henry clambered over the rubble and bounded up

105

the steps and onto the porch. He positioned himself in front of the door, spreading his arms and legs as wide as he possibly could.

"Orlando!" he yelled. "Are you there, Orlando? I need you now! The battle for Orozimbo has begun!"

He looked up at the excavator boom raised in the air, ready to strike an almighty blow. What was he doing? He decided that he was either very brave or completely stupid.

"Orlando!" he called again. "Where are you?" Where was a ghost when you needed one?

Henry held his breath. His heart pounded in his chest but he knew he couldn't move or the cottage would be lost. Would the driver see him in time? The platform swung around. The cab was now in clear view and he kept his gaze on the driver. The excavator boom started to move! The driver looked down at him in horror.

Henry heard the brakes hiss and the excavator stopped moving forward. He could see the driver yelling through the glass, but couldn't hear what he was saying over the noise of the engine. Now the man was making huge sweeping gestures with his arms, obviously signaling Henry to get out of the way.

Suddenly, Henry's father was by his side. In one smooth quick movement he grabbed him by the arms and dragged him off the front porch and away from the building towards where his mother was standing. Henry had never seen his father move that fast before.

His mother looked whiter than the ghosts he had just seen. "Henry! What possessed you to do that?" she yelled above the noise. "Are you trying to scare me? Are you trying to get yourself killed? You can't really hate this place that much!" She screamed at him, ranting on and on.

His father was panting heavily, hardly able to get out his words. "What . . . stupid . . . move . . . was that, son?" he finally asked. "Have you lost your mind completely?"

"I just wanted to save the front door," Henry answered. "And some of the old wood too-as a souvenir."

His mother's eyes looked like they might explode from their sockets. "What? You wanted to save some of it for a souvenir? I thought you hated the place!"

"That was before I found out about the history of Orozimbo," said Henry.

"Sometimes I just don't understand you!" His father threw up his hands. "You risked your life to save some rotten old wood that didn't even belong to the original house?"

"But it did!" shouted Henry. "I read that when Orozimbo was destroyed by the hurricane in 1932 they used the original wood from the old plantation home to build the cottage!"

His mother turned even whiter. Henry knew she loved history, and right from the first moment he had seen how much she loved Orozimbo. She would do anything to help preserve the past.

She sighed deeply. "Well, I wish you had told us that last night because it's too late to do anything now."

"But I only found out at midnight! That's why I couldn't get up this morning-I was up late reading about Orozimbo," said Henry as he watched the driver raise the boom once again. He bit his lips to stop them from quivering. "Goodbye, Orlando Phelps!" he mumbled. "Goodbye, Orozimbo!"

Suddenly there was an almighty clanking of grating metal. The tracks of the excavators kept slipping and refusing to move forward. The bucket at the end of the boom seemed to have a mind of its own, swinging up and down and banging the boom continuously. The platform of the excavator, along with the cab and the driver in it, rotated first in one direction and then in the other-back and forth, back and forth. Henry could see the driver in the cab screaming. The scene was like something out of a children's cartoon. Henry wanted to laugh, but was too stunned by what he was witnessing.

Then suddenly, Henry could hear more hissing

and grating noises behind him. He turned to see the guy in the bulldozer struggling with the controls. The bulldozer shunted around for a few seconds and then drove straight back up the ramp and onto the trailer! Just before it reached the cab, it came to a stop with a sudden massive shake.

"What the . . . ?" shouted Henry's father.

"What happened?" asked his mother. "Why did they stop the demolition?"

The driver of the excavator jumped down from the cab and came running. His face was drained of all color. "I'm sorry, ma'am. I don't think we'll be doing anything else today. Don't know what just happened. It's like the machine had a mind of its own. Something must be wrong with the controls."

The driver turned toward the bulldozer driver, who was standing on the bed of the trailer next to the bulldozer.

The bulldozer driver shrugged and said, "Nothing like this has ever happened before. Now I can't even get the 'dozer to start! We'll have to come back with a maintenance crew in a day or two. I'm sorry, but I don't think we'll be able to start again until Monday."

Henry felt unbelievable relief and incredible excitement all at once. He was certain he knew what had just happened, even if no one else did. Orlando Phelps had saved the day and they had just won a battle at Orozimbo!

Henry was so happy that he almost skipped back to the cabin.

"Show me what you were reading about Orozimbo's history, Henry," said his mother as she opened the front door.

Henry ran into the bedroom and quickly pulled the article about the Hounds of Orozimbo from the folder and tucked it away in his backpack. The last thing he wanted right now was to start a discussion about ghosts. He decided it would be best to stick to the historical facts if he wanted his mother's help.

He plunked the folder down on the kitchen table in front of her.

Her eyes widened. "Wow, Henry! Where did you get all of this?"

"Emily and I went to the Brazoria County Historical Museum on Monday morning. They told us lots of things about Orozimbo and copied all of these newspaper articles for us."

"I'm impressed," she said, looking through the folder. "For someone who never seemed interested in history, you've really gotten into this."

"I've divided up all the stories," said Henry pointing to the two paper-clipped stacks. "This pile is all about the Phelps family and these, in the back, are all about Santa Anna."

The Ghosts of Orozimbo

"I knew that Santa Anna was held prisoner here, but I had no idea we had a historical marker on the property," she said, looking at a photograph.

"Emily and I found it near the cottage. It's overgrown with weeds, but it's in great shape and you can still read it."

His father moved in closer and looked over his mother's shoulder at the photograph. "Henry, I'm so glad that you listened to me when I told you that this place had an amazing history, because now you are teaching us things! I think we should tape that marker off this afternoon. We don't want the bulldozers rolling over it on Monday!"

His mother picked up a piece of paper and read, "The Phelps house was destroyed by a hurricane in 1932 and by 1936 only a cottage made from the original timbers remained at the site."

"See," said Henry. "The wood in that cottage is 190 years old! It's surely worth saving a bit of it."

His mother stood up and walked to the nearest window in silence. She looked down the trail towards the cottage and then turned and said, "I have a brilliant idea. Why don't we use some of the original timbers ourselves?"

"Really?" said Henry. "You would do that?"

"Sure," she said beaming at him. "We're building our house to look like the original house anyway, so why not?"

"I think it's a great idea," agreed his father. "We could save some of the better wood from the cottage and build it into one of the new walls. That way we will be preserving a piece of our Texas heritage."

His mother seemed quite excited. "We could even put a special plaque on the wall, telling the story of Orozimbo and marking the wall of the house as historical," she added.

Henry felt like shouting for joy. "Thanks, Mom and Dad," he said, giving each of them a hug.

"We've got a couple of days to sort through the wood before they start demolition again," said his mother. "We can pile up all the pieces worth saving behind the cabin, ready for when they start construction. I hope there will be enough."

"We'll start after lunch!" said his father, who always loved a project. "There's a nice breeze today, and there's not a lot else we can do while we wait for the machinery to be repaired."

"Sounds good to me," said Henry.

He cleared away the newspaper articles and took them back to his room. It was then that he remembered what he had written as number 1 on his list about ghosts: Ghosts usually have unfinished business that they must resolve before they can leave Earth and cross into the light.

The Ghosts of Orozimbo

He couldn't wait to find Orlando again. If Orlando knew that Orozimbo would be preserved forever, that might help him cross into the light and rest in peace. But he also knew that Orlando and Santa Anna had unfinished business-and that needed resolving too!

Chapter 11

Henry woke up refreshed for the first time in nearly two weeks. He threw back the sheet and leaped out of bed. Today he had plans and he was eager to get started. Somehow he had to find Orlando again.

"We're going to get supplies from town and pick up Emily. Are you coming?" his mom called.

Henry walked into the kitchen where she was scribbling a list. "Nah, I think I'll stay here."

She looked wide-eyed. "Wow, Henry! I think Orozimbo must be growing on you. By the time our house is finished, you may actually like living here!"

Henry watched his parents get into the car and drive away. It seemed to take forever for the car to crawl down the long driveway and reach the gate. The moment the Explorer was out of sight and he was sure that his parents had truly left the plantation, he threw on his clothes, grabbed the roll of architect's plans off the kitchen table and headed down the steps.

Henry was convinced that he now had a good solution to his ghost problem. "Orlando!" he called excitedly, before he even reached the door of the cottage. "Orlando, can you hear me?"

Today there was less rubble to maneuver. He and his parents had worked hard yesterday afternoon sorting out any planks of wood worth saving. Now there was a huge stack of timber next to the cabin. Henry could hardly believe what they had achieved in just a few hours. His parents had even decided to get the builders to take down one of the remaining walls piece by piece, rather than let the excavator demolish it. The wall was in such a good shape that his parents had decided it was worth preserving.

They hadn't removed the door. There it still stood, eerily unsupported on each side-a gateway to nowhere. Henry had asked his parents if they could leave it for the builders to take down. He used the excuse that it was too heavy for them to lift over the rubble. But of course, he really wanted to see Orlando one more time and he couldn't wait to tell him about the plans for the new house.

Henry was about to do his usual leap onto the front porch when suddenly Orlando appeared in front of him.

"Ahhh!" he screamed, staggering backwards. "Don't do that!"

"I'm sorry, I didn't mean to startle you," said Orlando. "But you called me!"

Henry was shocked. Did Orlando just apologize for scaring him? That was a change from the aggressive behavior of before! He looked up at Orlando in the bright sunlight. What he had read about ghosts seemed to be true. This was the fourth time he had seen Orlando and this time his face had the look of a living person. Orlando had color in his cheeks and his lips were fleshy instead of taut.

"I thought I had to go through the door to get you to appear," said Henry, realizing that Orlando was not carrying a rifle.

Orlando actually smiled. "No," he said. "I just wanted to show you what Orozimbo was like when I was a young boy. You have to come through the door to see my wonderful childhood home, but I can appear to you in any place and at any time that I choose."

"Oh, of course," said Henry, remembering that they had first met on the trail by the clearing.

"Walk through the door and I'll show you more of Orozimbo," Orlando said, dissolving straight into the wood panels of the door!

"Whoa! What just happened? Where did you go?"

Henry was still caught off guard by this amazing ghostly ability. He presumed that Orlando would be waiting for him on the other side.

He turned the brass knob one more time and the door swung open. This time, he stepped into the house without worrying. For a few dizzying seconds Henry felt disoriented but then he clearly saw Orlando.

"Come this way," Orlando said, leading Henry across the entrance hall and into the kitchen. It was a cold room and Henry wasn't sure if that was because of the tiled floor or because he was in the presence of ghost. The large fireplace on the far wall was empty except for some charred logs left over from the last fire.

"Sit," said Orlando, pointing to the huge wooden kitchen table in the center of the room.

Henry looked at the rustic kitchen chairs. There were four along each side of the table and one at each end. He pulled one out and sat down, surprised by how comfortable they were.

"Thanks for your help yesterday," he said to Orlando. "I know it was you that made all the excavating equipment go crazy." Henry laughed. "It was pretty funny to watch."

"You did a brave thing for me, Henry Garrison, like a brother would. Now you understand that even though Orozimbo has fallen, it is still here within these timbers and needs protecting for all time. The memories and the history can never be replaced."

"I will protect it so that you can rest," said Henry. "I will-I swear."

"How so, Henry? How can you do that for me?"

"Don't get mad again, but my family really does own Orozimbo and I have a way to save it forever."

"My family still owns Orozimbo," said Orlando, raising his voice a little.

Henry sighed. "How can I make you understand?"

"It is you that doesn't understand, Henry Garrison. I told you that we have a deeper connection than I first thought. You are my family and so my family still owns Orozimbo."

Henry was completely baffled by that comment. Family? Probably because Orlando considered him a brother after he had stood in front of the excavator yesterday to protect the cottage. He decided not to press the issue of ownership for now. Instead he moved on to explain his solution.

"My parents are going to build our house to look just like the original Orozimbo plantation home." Henry unrolled the plans and spread them out on the table. "See . . . it looks just like it did when you lived here before the hurricane ripped it apart. It will have the same two huge front porches that you say you loved to sit on, a wonderful big fireplace like this one and lots of windows. And maybe I could suggest some red tile for the kitchen floor like you have. I will even ask my parents to put a clock in the hallway like the one that you showed to me."

Orlando studied the plans for a long time without saying a word. Finally he nodded. "I must admit, it looks the same."

"And now for the best news of all," said Henry. "We have saved the wood from the cottage that isn't rotten or doesn't have woodworm. It is stacked up behind our cabin. You should see how much we collected yesterday afternoon. It's a huge pile! My parents are going to use the original timber to build one wall of the new house. There will be a plaque on the wall telling people the history of Orozimbo plantation. So we really are saving Orozimbo forever."

Orlando looked radiant. "Thank you, Henry. It is a good solution, indeed! You have made me very happy. I will allow you to live at Orozimbo in peace and I know you will be honorable and protect it for the family."

The family? thought Henry. He pursed his lips, deciding that it was better not to risk angering him again. It was obvious, however, that Orlando still thought Orozimbo belonged to his family. Did it matter? He decided that it didn't, as long as Orlando wasn't going to threaten him to leave the property anymore. Henry rolled the plans up tightly and slipped the rubber band over the end.

"I can't thank you enough for standing with me, Henry, to fight for Orozimbo. But I hope you realize it was only the beginning. That was just the first battle. Now I must continue to prepare my troops for the next. You and I must fight Santa Anna for Orozimbo and then for the rest of Texas!"

"But Orlando . . ." said Henry, standing up.

"I must go immediately. Time is short. Santa Anna's men arrived by boat on the Brazos the last time they attacked this plantation. I must make sure our river defense is good."

"But I don't think Santa Anna . . ." began Henry, but Orlando was already gone, disappearing into thin air right in front of his eyes. "Orlando . . . wait! Come back!" Henry called after him. He wanted to tell him that Texas had been independent for well over 150 years and that these days Texans and Mexicans lived peacefully side by side. But it was too late. Orlando had presumably gone off to wage war.

Now Henry was really worried. Had he just set the wheels in motion for a bloody battle on Orozimbo soil?

He sauntered back to the cabin in the afternoon sun, put the plans back on the kitchen table and poured himself an ice-cold lemonade from the fridge. The cool drink slipped down his throat and calmed him. But then he remembered Orlando's words, "You and I must prepare to fight Santa Anna."

You and I? Did Orlando really expect Henry to be there fighting as well? This was not good at all. He needed to stop Orlando from fighting Santa Anna! Perhaps if he could find out why Santa Anna wanted to see Orlando, he could prevent a ghostly war.

Henry could hear car doors slam. His parents had returned. He looked at his watch. Was it 2 p.m. already? He hadn't even had time for lunch.

"Hey, Henry, I'm back!" Emily shouted before the front door was even ajar.

"Boy, am I glad to see you!" said Henry, ushering her into the other room, out of earshot of his parents.

Her eyes lit up. She threw her bag down on the bed. "What's up? What've I missed? Tell me quickly! I'll bet you've seen Orlando or those ghost hounds again!"

"So you read the story of The Hounds of Orozimbo, Em?"

"Of course, I did, and I believe you. I'll bet that's what you saw. It's exactly how you described those dogs to me."

"And they appeared on a really rainy night and when there was no moon," added Henry. "Just like the newspaper article said."

"It seems like Orozimbo is even more haunted than we thought! It's haunted by dog ghosts as well as human ghosts."

Henry didn't need to be reminded of that fact. "But, Em, don't you see? The dogs were not trying to get me at all. They were trying to get Santa Anna, or maybe even warn me about Santa Anna."

"You think?"

"Yeah, I do. And I've talked to Orlando again since you left-twice, in fact!"

"Did he threaten you again?"

Henry shook his head. "Nah, Orlando and I are cool."

"Cool? You are? Wow! That's a big difference! So, did he give you any clues about where to find the gold?"

"I asked him about the gold and-"

"Oh, this is so exciting!" Emily cut in. "Let's go look for it."

"There's no gold, Em . . . he told me that."

"Aww . . . are you sure? He's probably just saying that so you won't look for it."

"Nah. He's not trying to scare me off Orozimbo for the gold-I'm convinced. It's really all about protecting what he thinks is his family's property."

"But it's just a bunch of trees and a heap of rubble. The house has gone."

"It hasn't . . . completely."

"Huh?"

"I don't think he'll bother me anymore. I found a solution that made him happy. I'll explain everything on the way. Right now, we have a real problem to solve."

"Where are we going?"

"We've got to find Santa Anna, and fast. When I told Orlando that Santa Anna was here looking for him, he went into battle mode!"

"Battle mode? What does that mean?"

"He's preparing to fight a battle against Santa Anna to save Orozimbo-and he thinks I am going to help him!"

"Henry Garrison, just what have you gotten yourself into?"

Chapter 12

Henry led the way down to the Brazos River. Since arriving at Orozimbo he'd been so occupied with the dilapidated cottage that he hadn't yet explored this unbeaten path.

He and Emily had doused themselves in bug spray before they set off and yet still the mosquitoes seemed to find Henry's flesh. Occasionally they had to clamber over trees that had fallen across the trail and even in the thick undergrowth Palmetto palms were thriving. This habitat was a little different from the rest of the property with its scrubby bushes, huge oak trees and Spanish moss.

Henry trampled down some of the undergrowth. His fear that someone or something might suddenly appear had lessened, but he was still very concerned about the overall situation.

"El Presidente!" Emily called.

"He's not coming," said Henry, hoping that was true. If Santa Anna didn't appear then there could be no battle!

The Brazos River appeared as a shimmer of blue through the trees. It looked beautiful before they could even see it fully. As they got closer, the vegetation lessened, the trees thinned and finally they came upon its narrow muddy banks.

Henry stood there in silence. Emily didn't speak either. The setting was breathtaking. The sound of the rippling water was calming after the events of the last few days. It seemed so inviting on a hot afternoon.

"Wish we'd put swimsuits on," said Emily.

"So do I," said Henry, and for a moment he seriously considered taking off his socks and shoes and wading in.

"Do you hear something?" asked Emily, breaking into his thoughts.

Henry listened hard. It sounded like distant drums . . . and was that a fife he heard playing? "You're right, Em. They're coming."

"Who's coming-the Mexicans or the Texans?"

Henry shrugged. "Dunno." For once he wished he had studied history more. Perhaps then he would know how each army had marched into battle and the kind of music they had played. "Is the sound coming from down the river or from behind us?"

They both turned away from the banks and stared back up the trail in the direction of the cabin.

"I think it's Orlando and his men. The drums are definitely coming from the plantation, not the river," said Henry.

"If there's going to be a battle, do you think we should hide?" asked Emily.

"Not sure," said Henry, realizing it was the first time that Emily seemed nervous about the situation they were in.

Henry felt a sharp prod in the back. He froze, instinctively knowing that it was the barrel of a gun! His heart quickened and he wished he could run, but it was too late.

"Ahhh!" Emily screamed.

Henry guessed she had felt the gun too. "Em . . . stay still!" he whispered.

"No se mueven!" someone said in a loud voice.

Henry didn't understand what was said, but he raised his hands slowly in the air, figuring that was the sensible thing to do. Emily did the same.

"Date la vuelta lentamente!"

"I don't understand what you're saying!" Emily's voice trembled.

Henry decided that he had better translate what

Emily had just said.

"No lo entiendo," he said, using what little Spanish he knew.

"Turn around slowly," responded a deep voice with a heavy accent.

Henry and Emily shuffled slowly around, their hands still in the air, until they were facing the river. They gasped, in unison.

At least twenty men, dressed in old-fashioned navy blue jackets and white pants, stood in two long lines along the bank, and all had their rifles pointed straight at them. Henry hesitated for a moment and then remembered he had seen these very same uniforms pictured on the internet. The men were Mexican military! Surely he and Emily would have heard twenty men sneak up behind?

Henry scanned the banks of the river. There were no boats moored anywhere close by! How did the soldiers get there? And so quietly!

It was then that he realized that the air had turned cold. In fact, the temperature had plunged to around freezing and yet it was another 95-degree day. As he studied the line of soldiers he could see that they all had pasty white complexions and their faces seemed elongated.

"Ghosts!" he whispered to Emily. Of course they were ghosts! Isn't that what he and Emily had come in search of? Why else would there be twenty armed Mexican soldiers on his property?

Henry wondered if ghost rifles could actually fire! He had just assumed Orlando's rifle would fire, but now he wasn't so sure. Was it wise to take the chance? He was sweating in spite of the chilly temperature and could feel the perspiration dripping from his hair line all the way down his cheeks and down his back. Ghosts or not, this was a desperate situation.

"Please . . . we're not armed," was all he could think to say.

Out of the shadow of a cypress tree hobbled Santa Anna, using a crutch to support himself. He motioned for his men to lower their weapons.

Henry felt overwhelming relief as he heard the distinctive 'click click' of the bolts going back and the rifles being disarmed. He'd been deer hunting with his dad a few times and had learned a lot about gun safety.

"El Presidente!" said Henry.

"Thank goodness it's you!" Emily cried.

Santa Anna used his crutch to move closer. "Mi cosa dulce . . . my sweet one," he said, looking at Emily. "I'm sorry if my men frightened you. And I see that the boy, Henry, is with you again. Did you give my message to Orlando?"

"Yes, El Presidente," said Henry, still a little fearful.

"Did you tell him I was looking for him?"

"Ummm . . . yes, sir, we did," Henry answered. "But Orlando thinks you want to do battle for Orozimbo."

An expression of alarm crossed Santa Anna's face. "He does? And what makes him think that?"

"We didn't know why you wanted to see him and so he's gathering his men to be prepared."

Henry noticed that the sounds of the drums had grown considerably louder.

"Is that Orlando I hear coming?" asked Santa Anna.

Henry nodded. "I think it's Captain Orlando Phelps with the Alamo Militia."

"Los hombres! Ocultar!" bellowed Santa Anna. His men immediately ran for cover behind the trees.

Santa Anna hobbled after them.

Henry and Emily were left standing alone on the banks of the river.

"What do we do, Henry?" Emily questioned.

"Dunno," said Henry. "I guess we stand here and wait."

"But then we'll be in the middle of the battle!"

The heavy marching beat of the drums grew louder and the light cheery melody of the fifes intensified.

Emily grabbed on to Henry's arm. "I really think we should hide," she said adamantly.

The Texas Lone Star flag came into view, flapping madly in the breeze. But it seemed to be floating in mid air! Where were the militia? Henry couldn't see even one man holding a drum or a fife. The instruments looked as though they were floating on their own!

"Orlando and even more ghosts," Emily whispered, stating the obvious.

Then, as if by magic, Orlando appeared in front of them. He was followed by the flag bearer and a line of men carrying drums and fifes. Closely behind marched his militia, clutching rifles and dressed in an assortment of clothing.

Henry thought fast. Shivering, he stripped off his white T-shirt and waved it in the air, shouting. "Orlando! Stop there! Don't come any closer!"

Orlando held up his hand and his men came to a grinding halt. They spread out and took a defensive position across the trail and into the undergrowth on either side.

Henry turned to see Santa Anna's men slip out from behind the trees. They stood facing Orlando's men with their rifles aimed and ready.

Orlando looked horrified. "My brother, what are

you doing with the Mexicans? Have you betrayed me, Henry Garrison?"

"N-n-no," Henry stammered. "You know I am your brother and I wouldn't do that."

Henry and Emily stood between the two groups. Henry had no idea what would happen next, but he continued to wave the white shirt.

"Santa Anna only wants to talk to you, Orlando," he bellowed. "He is not here for a fight. I'll stay here in between both armies. You should each walk forward and meet me here in the middle."

"How can we trust that Santa Anna's men won't open fire?" shouted Orlando.

"Because I am risking my life by standing in between you," said Henry.

"In fact, where is General Santa Anna?" Orlando questioned. "What kind of leader is he, that he hides while his men to do battle for him?"

Santa Anna hobbled into view using his crutch. "As you can see, Orlando, I am in no state to run from your army. Why would I come to do battle with one leg and no horse to help me escape?"

Now Orlando looked shocked. "So be it. I will meet you for discussion with my brother, Henry." He placed his weapon slowly on the ground, whispered something to one of his men and began to walk forward slowly, in time with the drum beat.

For Henry, it seemed to take the longest time for the two leaders to approach. He watched their men for signs that they would not obey orders, but none of them so much as flinched.

Finally Santa Anna and Orlando Phelps stood face to face. They bowed to each other.

"Orlando, surely you know that I would not come here to harm you or your family," said Santa Anna. "I owe my life to your family and would never take Orozimbo from them."

"Yet your men still cross the border and invade our small towns and our forts, even though peace treaties were signed and the Republic of Texas has been annexed by the United States."

"There will be peace," said Santa Anna.

"There is peace," said Henry loudly, but his words seemed to fall on deaf ears. The two men were completely engrossed in their conversation.

"I am not here to fight you. I came to ask you a favor, Orlando."

"What could I possibly do for El Presidente?" asked Orlando.

"Help me find my leg!"

In that moment, Santa Anna seemed so small and vulnerable.

Orlando's mouth dropped open. He looked at a loss for words and the corners of his mouth twitched as though he was about to break into laughter. Finally Orlando said, "Your real leg or your wooden leg, General?"

"Both have been stolen from me!"

Henry felt a flood of mixed emotions. Now he wanted to laugh! Here was the infamous fearless, brutal Santa Anna looking for his leg . . . any leg-real or otherwise! It seemed quite comical. But of course it was really quite sad at the same time.   Henry reminded himself that this was potentially an explosive situation with two armies ready to do battle!   He managed to stifle his smirk.

"I have given up finding my real leg, so I cannot rest in peace until I find my wooden leg," continued El Presidente.

"What happened to your real leg?" asked Henry.

"My real leg was blown off by the French not long after I signed the Treaties of Velasco. We had a proper burial for my leg and it was laid to rest at the Pantheon of Saint Paula in Mexico."

Emily looked at Henry, the most horrified expression on her face, and he knew exactly what she was thinking. A burial ceremony for a leg? How odd! They had never heard of such a thing!

"But my own people stole my leg from the tomb two years later during riots in Mexico," continued Santa Anna. "I have not seen it since then and no one knows where it is."

"He already had a wooden leg when he let me go after the Battle at Mier," added Orlando.

"That wooden leg was very special to me. It was carved out of the finest oak and cork and it was taken by American soldiers!"

"How?" asked Henry.

"I was sitting under a tree eating lunch during a battle . . . in 1847, I think . . . and I had removed my leg to be more comfortable. I was ambushed by American soldiers from the 4th Illinois Infantry who had come onto Mexican soil. In my hurry to escape, I galloped off without it!"

Emily giggled under her breath.

Henry prayed that Santa Anna hadn't heard her. It took all of his effort to keep a serious expression. "Can't you have another one made?" he asked.

"I have had many different ones over the years, but that one was special. It was so beautifully carved. I cannot rest until I know where it is."

"If you can guarantee peace between our nations I will find out what happened to your leg," said Orlando, stretching out his hand to shake Santa Anna's.

Henry was stunned. This had turned into a comedy. But at least it seemed as though a battle had been avoided.

Suddenly there was an almighty howling through the trees. It sounded as though a pack of coyotes was about to descend upon them.

Henry couldn't move, suddenly paralyzed with fear. He knew the sound only too well. His heart thumped so heavily, it felt as though it was beating in his ears as well as his chest.

The horrific baying noise grew louder and louder.

The soldiers on both sides lifted their rifles, but they appeared to be unsure where to aim.

Henry and Emily turned in circles . . . watching . . . . waiting . . .

There was tension in the air, and Henry prayed that the armies wouldn't shoot at each other in their confusion and panic.

It was Orlando who finally said what they already knew. "It's the Hounds of Orozimbo . . . they're coming!"

Chapter 13

The long doleful sounds of the dogs sent chills down Henry's spine, and now he began to second guess his earlier conclusion. What if he'd been wrong? What if the dogs were coming for him after all? "I thought that the Hounds of Orozimbo only came out on rainy, moonless nights," he said, his voice quaking.

"Not if their prey is in sight," said Orlando, looking straight at the Mexican army. "They want revenge for the killing of their old master at Goliad, and they are here to protect me as their new master."

Henry swallowed hard. Orlando's words offered some comfort, but still he felt unsure. He'd never forget the snarling dogs with their vicious bared teeth that had greeted him at the window several nights before.

The howling continued.

Santa Anna looked very uncomfortable. He scanned the trees nervously.

Henry looked at Emily. "I think we'll be okay," he said, shuffling uneasily from foot to foot. "Let's stand close to Orlando . . . just in case."

Emily nodded and grabbed Henry's hand.

The baying became louder. The dogs were definitely close. The Mexican soldiers panicked and began to run. They scattered in all directions, screaming and climbing trees.

"Stay and protect El Presidente!" Santa Anna bellowed at his men, but none obeyed.

Even Orlando's men looked nervous. He tried to reassure them, but many stood with their backs to the trees, as if a large trunk could protect them from a wild dog.

Suddenly, the baying became deafening and out of nowhere, three huge dogs leaped through the branches and into the clearing. They sprang at some of the Mexican soldiers, sinking their claws into their chests. Shrill cries reverberated through the woods.

Santa Anna screamed as the pink hairless dog bounded straight for him, teeth bared, growling angrily.

"Get away! Get away!" he bellowed, whilst trying to battle the dog with his crutch.

The dog went after Santa Anna's good leg, knocking him to the ground.

"Ahhh!" Santa Anna yelled in pain as the dog sank his teeth into his leg.

Orlando jumped onto the back of the dog and wrestled him, shouting, "Stop! No more! Your master's life has been avenged! The Mexicans are not here to kill me and my men."

The dog seemed to understand. He immediately released his clenched jaws from Santa Anna's thigh and howled loudly. The other two glowing white hounds also stopped attacking the Mexican soldiers. They backed away, their heads down and tails between their legs.

All three dogs sat in front of Orlando, whimpering.

"Your old master did not die in vain," said Orlando to the dogs. "He gave his life for a just cause. You hounds have protected me well for many years here at Orozimbo, and for that I am grateful. Peace will now reign, Texas will be free of Mexican control and Orozimbo will be a part of that glorious history forever. Your job is done and it is time for you to rest."

Henry could feel his pulse slow and Emily released her grip on his hand.

Orlando bent down and patted each dog on the head in turn. "Now go!" he ordered.

Suddenly a low fog drifted in, like a thick cloud, clinging to the ground. It was so thick that Henry couldn't even see his feet. It thinned, drifted in wisps through the trees and finally up to the sky. When it cleared, the Hounds of Orozimbo were gone.

Henry sighed heavily. The worst was over. There had been no battle, the dogs were gone and Orlando had saved Santa Anna. He felt pleased and relieved-it was a very successful outcome to a very bad situation.

"It seems that I am eternally in debt to your family, Orlando Phelps," said Santa Anna, who was groaning in agony on the ground.

Orlando helped him sit upright. "You repaid that debt with your kindness to me when I was captured in Mexico," said Orlando, "and I will never forget that. But you still owe a debt to all my compatriots who have died in battle. You must honor your agreements made at Velasco and let Texans live in peace."

"This is the end of all hostilities," said Santa Anna. "The war is over."

Henry walked over to help. Together, he and Orlando lifted Santa Anna to his feet and propped him against a tree trunk.

"Thank you. I will be fine," he said, although there was a huge open wound in his leg.

Henry was fascinated to see that there was no sign of any blood on Santa Anna. He decided that when this was all over he would do more research on ghosts.

"I will do what I can to find your wooden leg," said

Orlando. "I will send my men to talk to the different infantry regiments that were involved in the skirmish the day your leg was taken."

Emily walked over to Santa Anna. "We'll help too-Henry and I know very fast ways to find out information."

Santa Anna smiled at her in a condescending way and Henry realized that he was probably thinking that a young girl could be of little help. But of course he had no knowledge of the internet.

"We'll start looking immediately," said Henry.

"Gracias," said Santa Anna.

"Henry, I thank you too," said Orlando. "You have honored your family by your bravery in protecting Orozimbo today."

Henry grabbed Emily by the arm and led her down the trail. They walked a few steps and turned to wave goodbye, but the bank of the river was already deserted. There was no sign of Santa Anna, Orlando Phelps or any of their men.

Henry stood staring at the rippling water for a few minutes. "Did that really just happen?" he said to Emily.

"Well, it did for me," she acknowledged. "So I don't think two of us could have been dreaming."

"It all seems so unreal," said Henry beginning the walk back to the cabin.

"Ghosts aren't real humans," said Emily. "Well, at least not any more."

"No one would ever believe me," said Henry. "The whole thing sounds so crazy!"

"You said yourself that ghosts have unresolved issues. Everything fits together. Orlando wanted to protect the old plantation house from being destroyed, the Hounds of Orozimbo wanted revenge for the killing of their master at Goliad and were there to protect Orlando from Santa Anna, and Santa Anna can't rest until he finds his leg."

"Yeah, the leg is the last unresolved problem. Then perhaps they will all leave me alone!" said Henry.

They climbed the steps to the cottage, and said a quick few words to Henry's parents who were sitting on the front porch swing.

Henry went straight into the bedroom and pulled out the folder of information. "Here, Em. You can wade through this lot to see if there's any information about Santa Anna's leg and I'll use my phone to search the internet."

"Sure." She sat down on the bed with the open folder in front of her. Henry left her reading and walked to the kitchen window with his iPhone. He barely had 3G today. As he sat at the kitchen table waiting for the slow connection to Google he realized that there were other important questions nagging in the back of his mind. Why did Orlando still think that Orozimbo was owned by the Phelps family and that Henry was part of that family?

Henry popped his head round the screen door and said, "Mom, we're not related to the Phelps family who used to own Orozimbo, are we?"

His mother looked up from her book. She frowned. "I don't think so, Henry. Why do you ask?"

"Oh, I just wondered," he responded and ducked back inside.

Henry realized that Google had now loaded. He had just finished entering General Antonio Lopez de Santa Anna, missing leg, when he heard a shriek from the bedroom.

"Henry! Look what I've found out!" Emily came running into the kitchen waving a sheet of paper madly in the air. "Read this story about Santa Anna's captivity at Orozimbo."

Henry began reading. The name Mrs. Almira Phelps Garrison instantly got his attention. "Garrison?" said Henry out aloud. "She has my last name . . ."

"Read on!" Emily said excitedly.

The newspaper story had been written years before. Mrs. Garrison, an old lady, said that she remembered being told as a child that her grandfather, Dr. James Aeneas Phelps, had saved Santa Anna's

143

life with a stomach pump.

Henry nearly fell off the kitchen chair when he realized the implication of what he had just read. "So, if Almira Garrison was the granddaughter of Dr. James Phelps, then who was her father? Do you think it was Orlando?"

"Google her, quick!" said Emily.

Henry instantly got his answer. Almira Phelps: born in West Columbia, married Henry Garrison. Daughter of Orlando C. Phelps.

There on the screen was the confirmation he needed. So that was why Orlando considered Henry to be his family! Orlando obviously thought that Henry was a descendant of the Henry Garrison who had married his daughter, and that was the deeper connection he had been talking about!

"Henry Garrison! Can you believe it? Isn't that cool!" said Emily.

"Henry Garrison was born in 1864, married Almira in 1890 and died in 1928," said Henry, reading more information on his iPhone. "That's weird."

"Why?"

"Because last time I was with Orlando in the house he thought he was 25 years old battling Santa Anna in 1847! His daughter was not yet born when he was that age, and yet he thinks I am a descendent of his daughter and son-in-law."

"I read somewhere that ghosts have no concept of time. So maybe now that he's a ghost, the years have all run together," said Emily. "Orozimbo connects all of these historical events together."

"So you think Orlando is in limbo, trying to protect Orozimbo."

"You know, you might actually be the great, great, great grandson of Henry Garrison."

"Our fathers are brothers, so that would mean that you would be related to him as well!" said Henry.

Emily giggled. "That would be so cool!"

"Nah." Henry shook his head. "My mom doesn't think we're related to the Phelps family at all, but I'll get my parents to check out our family tree on dad's side sometime."

Emily sucked in a deep breath. "Hey, you're not going to tell Orlando that you're probably not related to him, are you?"

"No way!" replied Henry. "I wouldn't want to risk making him mad again. Even if I'm not a true relation, Orlando says I am his brother-in-arms because I defended Orozimbo."

"Let's hope that's good enough," said Emily.

Henry picked up his iPhone again. "I was just looking for information about Santa Anna's leg when you screamed."

"Oh!" said Emily. "I was so excited, I almost forget!

I found stuff about that too!"

She ran across the room, tripping on the rug in her eagerness. A minute later she was back with the folder. "There are three pages about his leg. It is perfectly safe."

"How do you mean safe?" asked Henry. He took the papers from her.

"Well, no one is going to take it because it's in a special display in the Illinois National Guard Museum in central Illinois. See, there's even a photograph of his leg," said Emily.

Henry looked at the photo of an elaborately carved wooden leg wearing a black boot.

"Let's go and tell Santa Anna!" said Henry.

"What . . . right now? Haven't you had enough ghosts for one day?"

"I want to get this finished with so that I can get on with my life," said Henry.

"You won't be in such a hurry to see Santa Anna when you realize we've got a major problem," said Emily.

"Problem? What major problem?"

"Santa Anna wants his leg back. But he can't have it back now that it's in a museum!"

Chapter 14

Henry was a little anxious about breaking the news about the leg to Santa Anna, but more than that he felt he felt a real mixture of emotions. He wanted to get back to a normal life, but at the same time he felt an overwhelming sadness. He had been terrified of encounters with ghosts and yet now he realized that he didn't really want them to stop. This could be the last time that he saw Orlando Phelps or Santa Anna. Wasn't that what he had wanted-Orlando and Santa Anna gone from Orozimbo?

He stood with Emily on the concrete slab of the cottage, surrounded by a couple of dilapidated walls, broken windows and the door that seemed to support itself.

On Monday the bulldozers and excavators would

be back and the cottage would all be gone, ready for a new house to take its place. He knew that it had to happen, but now he realized that he had grown to love the pile of rubble and all the adventures that it had brought.

He sat down on some of the remaining rotten floorboards. Throughout most of the cottage the concrete slab had already been revealed underneath.

Emily sat next to him, fidgeting. For once she seemed more nervous than him. "So do we just sit here and wait?"

"I guess we could call them," Henry replied. "But I don't think we'll need too," he added, suddenly feeling cold. The chilled feeling could only mean one thing. He prepared himself for what was probably going to be his last meeting with the ghosts of Orozimbo.

"There's certainly no need to call me," said a deep voice. "I am already here."

Henry's heart skipped a beat. He looked up to see Orlando towering over them.

"I fear I have had no luck tracing Santa Anna's leg," said Orlando. "None of my men were at the border that day, and none of them have heard any details of the incident from the other regiments. I am at a loss as to what to try next." said Orlando.

Henry stood up and brushed his hands together to

remove the dust. "You needn't worry. We've got news for El Presidente."

"We have found his wooden leg," said Emily more quietly than usual.

As if by magic, Santa Anna was suddenly standing next to Orlando. "Emily, mi cosa dulce . . . you have information for me?"

Henry couldn't help but smile. The emphasis on the word you confirmed what he had thought earlier-that Santa Anna didn't believe for one minute that Emily could help him find his leg.

"So, where is it? Tell me quickly, so I can get it back," he continued.

Henry gulped. How would Santa Anna react when he discovered that the leg, although safe, was beyond his reach? This man could be ruthless and cruel even to his friends. Would he haunt Henry forever?

Emily trembled as she handed him the printed sheet of information and the photograph. "Is this your wooden leg?" she asked.

Santa Anna muttered a few words in Spanish as he read the page.

Henry held his breath.

After what seemed like an eternity, Santa Anna looked up. He wasn't smiling.

"So my leg is in a museum, miles away from here in a place called Illinois?"

Now Emily looked frightened. "Umm . . . yes . . . El Presidente."

"And just how am I supposed to get it back?" he bellowed.

Orlando took two steps backward and clenched his rifle, as if fearful that Santa Anna would explode.

Henry looked at Santa Anna's angry expression. No longer did he have a pasty-white ghost-like complexion. Santa Anna looked as red in the face as Henry's father did when he was angry.

Henry moved in front of Emily . . . just in case. "You aren't going to get it back," he said bravely.

Santa Anna hobbled a dozen steps one way and then a dozen steps back again. "I will gather my men immediately. We will march to Illinois and do battle for my leg! Our numbers will overwhelm them."

Henry sighed. "El Presidente, sir, what you and Orlando don't seem to realize is that the war between Mexico and the Unites States ended more than 150 years ago. These days Texans go on vacation to Mexico!"

Santa Anna turned to Orlando, complete disbelief on his face. "Vacation? They go on vacation?"

"Yes, sir," continued Emily, finding her courage again. "Americans like to visit Mexico's beautiful beaches and the amazing Mayan ruins. Your leg is part of history. People from both countries can go to the museum in Illinois and read all about the battles between Texas and Mexico."

"You should be proud, sir," said Henry, trying desperately to make Santa Anna's leg being in a museum sound like a good thing.

"Proud?

"Yes, sir."

"How can I be proud that my leg is on display for all to see?"

"Because everyone can learn about General Antonio López de Santa Anna. They will know about the Battle of the Alamo and they will know how you were defeated at the Battle of San Jacinto. They will know about how you signed peace treaties at Velasco and how you were brought here to Orozimbo and held as a prisoner for five months."

"And how you were President of Mexico eleven times," Emily added quickly.

Henry smiled at her thankfully, realizing that he had been listing mostly the good things for Texas, but the bad things for Santa Anna.

"I see. So you are telling me that I am part of history?"

"Yes, El Presidente," said Emily. "You are in the history books. The museum in Illinois will tell that history to everyone who visits. Just look at how beautiful the diorama is in the photo. It's a full-sized model of your elegant carriage. Your leg is propped up in the carriage and it is surrounded by soldiers. And look, there are even some boxes of gold and a plate of chicken to show how you had to quickly leave your meal when the Texans arrived. It's a very interesting tale."

"Hmmm." A smile crept across Santa Anna's face. "So I, Napoleon of the West, am part of history, eh?"

Henry started to relax. "Yes, sir. You and Orlando both are."

Santa Anna's anger subsided. "So perhaps it is a good thing that my leg was stolen!"

"I think so," said Emily. "The story will be told forever."

Santa Anna seemed lost in thought for a moment. He folded the paper and stuffed it down the front of his brocaded jacket. "Thank you, mi cosa dulce. I like that I will be part of history and everyone will know how the American soldiers stole my leg. Now I will be able to rest."

Henry looked at Orlando, who had noticeably relaxed his grip on his rifle.

"Soon my parents will rebuild Orozimbo," said Henry. "Orlando, I promise you that we will use the original wood and it will be a part of history too. I'll make sure that the museum in Angleton knows everything about Orozimbo."

"Thank you, Henry," nodded Orlando. I know that our family history is in good hands. I will not bother you again. Goodbye, my brother."

Henry extended his hand to shake Orlando's but, as quick as a flash of lightning, Orlando and Santa Anna had both vanished.

"Wow! They've gone-just like that!" said Emily, snapping her fingers.

"And I don't think they'll be back," said Henry. He looked around. Yes, they were definitely gone, and instead of feeling relief, he felt empty deep inside.

"I'm gonna miss El Presidente," said Emily as they walked back to the cabin, "even if most people hated him."

"I'm not!" said Henry. "He frightened me. But I will miss Orlando."

They climbed up the steps of the front porch. Henry's parents came out to meet them. His mom was beaming.

"Glad you're both back before the light fades," she said. "We've got something incredible to show you."

"Oh? What?" asked Henry.

His parents led them back down the trail towards the ruins. Henry's father ran ahead and bent over close to the historical marker. He pulled some of the tall grass to one side.

"Come and see what I found, kids," he shouted as

they approached.

Henry ran to take a look. His heart skipped a beat as he peered into the grass. Lying on the ground was the grandfather clock that had once stood in the entrance hall of the old plantation home. "Wow! Where did that come from?"

"I've just found it," said his father. "And it looks to be in great shape."

"We've all walked through that grass so many times in the last week, I really don't know how we could have missed it before!" said his mother. "And how that giant excavator didn't smash it the other day, I just don't know!"

Emily came closer to take a look. "It is in very good condition. Do you think it still chimes?"

"It would be remarkable if it did, considering it's been lying out here in the grass," his mother said. "With a bit of polish it will look great in the entrance hall of our new house. Don't you think, Henry?"

Henry nodded. He was still in shock. The clock was definitely the one he'd heard chime loudly on his visits to old Orozimbo with Orlando-and it was definitely not lying there in the grass yesterday!

"Come on kids, let's get some dinner," said his mom. "The clock is too heavy for us to lift on our own. We'll end up damaging it."

"The builders can help us move it inside the cabin

on Monday," added his father as he walked away.

Henry felt a cold chill in the air, despite the heat of the late afternoon sun. His heart beat faster. He knew what the change in temperature meant, and looked quickly around. But Orlando didn't appear.

As he turned to leave he heard a faint whisper in his ear. "Henry . . . Henry Garrison . . . I hope you like my gift for the new Orozimbo! It is a connection to the past to remind you to protect my home forever."

Emily reached up to Henry's shoulders and shook him. "Hey, Henry . . . are you okay? Snap out of it! You look like you've just seen another ghost!"

"Didn't you hear him, Em?"

"Hear who?"

"Orlando!"

Emily looked quickly around. "No."

"The clock . . . it's a gift from Orlando!" said Henry. "He just told me!"

"Well, I didn't hear him. But I guess it makes sense . . . the clock certainly wasn't there before."

"Do you think my parents will let people tour the plantation and the new house so we can tell them the amazing history?"

"That would be so cool," said Emily. "That's a really great idea, but why would you want to do that? You've always hated history and you don't like Orozimbo either!"

"That was before I found my connection to the past," said Henry, thinking of Charlie and how right the old man had been. "Now I want to tell everyone about Orozimbo and Orlando C. Phelps."

"And don't forget El Presidente and the Hounds of Orozimbo," added Emily.

Henry chuckled. "I think I'm actually looking forward to moving here!"

"You could give ghost tours! People like to hear that a place is haunted and everyone loves a good ghost story!"

"Yeah, and you've got to admit that my stories are the best! Ghosts . . . right here on our land! Who ever would have guessed?"

"And so many of them all in one place! That's way cool!"

Henry sighed. "But the tours won't be the same without a real ghost sighting."

"You're right," said Emily in a sad tone. "There's nothing like a ghost sighting to get the tourists and ghost hunters coming. Maybe you could get some white dogs just for effect!"

Henry smiled at her. "Good idea, Em. Mom likes dogs, so I'm sure she'd say yes. Now that we've laid the ghosts of Orozimbo to rest, I really wish we hadn't!"

Emily brightened up. "You never know. Orlando

might come back to visit and there might still be some ghosts we haven't met!"

"Mom said there's a graveyard on the property where Dr. James Phelps is buried."

Emily clapped her hands together in excitement. "Really? Now you're talking, Henry! Tomorrow let's go and look for it. I don't think our ghost hunting days are over!"?

Above: The historical marker outside the museum in Surfside Beach, Texas

Below: City Hall, Surfside Beach (The Village of Surfside Beach Museum)
Photographs by H.J. Ralles

159

Orozimbo Plantation in the early 1900s
Image courtesy of the Brazoria County Historical Museum

Below: Part of Orozimbo Plantation today
Photo by H.J. Ralles

Above: The cottage and the historical marker at Orozimbo

Below: The Brazoria County Historical Museum, Angleton, Texas
Images courtesy of the Brazoria County Historical Museum

Part 2

The Real Story

of

Orozimbo

Orozimbo and the Phelps family

1936: Orozimbo in a state of disrepair
Image courtesy of the Brazoria County Historical Commission

Orozimbo Plantation was located near West Columbia, Brazoria County, Texas, nine miles northwest of Angleton.

The plantation was owned by Dr. James Aeneas Enos Phelps who came with his family to Texas from

Mississippi in 1822. He and his wife, Rosetta Yerby, had two sons and two daughters. Orlando Phelps was his oldest son. The Phelps family had one servant and fifteen slaves, which they brought with them from Mississippi.

Dr. Phelps acquired the land near West Columbia in 1824 and built a beautiful two-story white-frame house that he named Orozimbo after an Indian chief. The rafters that supported the roof were held together with wooden pegs instead of nails, typical of a house built back then.

Dr. Phelps was a hospital surgeon in the Texas Army at the Battle of San Jacinto in 1836. After the battle, however, he became better known for his treatment of General Santa Anna, who was held prisoner at Orozimbo for over five months.

James Phelps died in 1847 and is buried at Orozimbo. After his father's death Orlando Phelps lived at Orozimbo for many years before moving to Houston to live with his daughter. Records show that Orlando died in 1897 and is buried in Houston, but some people believe that he is buried alongside his father at Orozimbo.

Orozimbo flourished as a cotton plantation from colonial times until the Civil War. The Phelps family also owned 120 cattle.

In 1932 the Phelps house was destroyed by a

The Orozimbo Oak after fire destroyed it in 1981
Image courtesy of the Brazoria County Historical Museum

hurricane, and four years later the original timbers from Orozimbo were used to build a cottage on the site. Four cornerstones and a cistern still mark the footings of the original plantation house.

It is reported that the reason that the Phelps family chose the exact site for their home was because of a monster of an oak tree that provided the house with shade during the long hot summer months.

The Orozimbo Oak, as it became known, survived the hurricane but was finally destroyed by fire in 1981. Two teenage boys built a fire for warmth near the oak. Because of a high wind and holes in the hollow tree, it caught fire. The firemen on the scene said that flames reached 12 feet above the top of the tree and that it resembled a drilling rig on fire. They used over 8,000 gallons of water and still couldn't put out the fire.

Orozimbo and General Santa Anna

Antonio López de Santa Anna
public domain image

General Santa Anna was born on February 21, 1794. His full name was Antonio de Padua María Severino López de Santa Anna y Pérez de Lebrón.

Santa Anna was born into a wealthy family and attended school. He joined the Mexican army when he was only 16 years old and was promoted to captain six years later. He was president of Mexico eleven times

169

over a period of 22 years! At age 31, he married Ines Garcia and had four children; Guadalupe, María del Carmen, Manuel, and Antonio.

Although no one can deny that he was a brave soldier and a cunning politician, General Santa Anna is said to be the most hated person in Texas history and was also disliked by many Mexicans. He was sometimes called "the Napoleon of the West." He sought glory for himself, was a cruel and ruthless leader, and his military defeats resulted in Mexico losing over half its territory, including California, New Mexico, Nevada and Utah!

The Capture of General Santa Anna

After Santa Anna became president of Mexico in 1833, he became a dictator backed by the military and was very unpopular with the Mexican people. He replaced the Mexican constitution with "the seven laws." Several Mexican states hated the changes to the law and formed their own governments. Part of Coahuila y Tejas, one of those states, declared its independence from Mexico on March 2, 1836 and became the Republic of Texas.

Santa Anna believed that a show of brute force would bring Texas back under Mexican control and he headed north to the newly independent state.

Following a 13-day siege, the final assault of the Battle of the Alamo was fought on March 6, 1836. Santa Anna showed no mercy. His massive army killed 189 Texans and executed 342 prisoners. Just a few days later, 303 Texan soldiers were taken prisoner at Goliad, and upon Santa Anna's orders, all were executed–but 28 of them feigned death and managed to escape!

General Santa Anna
public domain image

Santa Anna was confident after winning these battles. However, his expedition ended tragically. He had recruited many Indians who did not speak Spanish and could not understand his commands; he had expected tropical weather in the Republic of Texas and instead his men suffered from the cold. His army lacked horses, mules, wagons, medical supplies and food and, when the water supply became contaminated, many of his men took ill.

The Ghosts of Orozimbo

General Sam Houston and his army finally defeated Santa Anna at the Battle of San Jacinto on April 21, 1836. The Texans shouted, "Remember Goliad, Remember the Alamo!" as they charged into battle.

The day after the battle, Santa Anna was captured by a small band of Texan soldiers on horseback. He was found hiding in a marsh, barefoot and dressed in a dragoon corporal's uniform. Under his arm was a tightly wrapped bundle.

The three men who captured Santa Anna did not recognize him. Believing him to be a regular Mexican soldier, they ordered him to surrender and threatened to kill him on the spot if he didn't march ahead of them towards the camp.

After Santa Anna had walked about half a mile he told the soldiers that he could not walk any farther because of his blistered feet. Two soldiers made a move to kill him, but the other, Joel Robison, was a kind man. He took Santa Anna's hand and helped him up on to his horse.

The Texan soldiers rode into camp with their prisoner. Santa Anna whispered to Joel Robison, in excellent English, asking that he be taken to see General Sam Houston. Joel then realized that he had a notorious prisoner sitting behind him. He feared that the Texans would kill Santa Anna if he were recognized, and so he rode rapidly to General Houston, who was lying wounded under an oak tree being treated by Dr. James Phelps.

The Surrender of Santa Anna - *public domain image*

Santa Anna surrendered to General Houston and asked for protection. He then thanked Joel Robison for saving his life and gave him the bundle he had been carrying. Inside was a vest adorned with rows of pure gold buttons and pants to match. Joel Robison took the jacket home with him and, for many years after that, the sons of the Robisons' neighbors wore Santa Anna's jacket at their weddings.

Santa Anna and the Treaties of Velasco

On April 28, 1836 General Antonio Lopez de Santa Anna, then 44 years old, was taken from San Jacinto to Galveston. Some people reported that he was calm and dignified; others said that he was crying.

A few days later President Burnet, the interim president of the Republic of Texas, his cabinet and Santa Anna boarded the Texas gunboat Invincible. On May 8, 1836, two weeks after the Battle of San Jacinto, Santa Anna arrived in Velasco, which at that time was a temporary capital of the Republic of Texas and is now called the City of Surfside Beach.

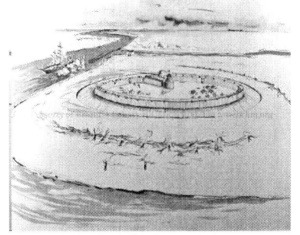

Artist sketch showing Fort Velasco
*Image courtesy of the Brazoria County Historical Commission
and to Artist Don Hutson*

President Burnet and his cabinet hammered out two treaties. The first, a public treaty between Mexico and Texas, stated that all hostilities were to cease against the Texans, prisoners were to be exchanged, and the Mexicans were to withdraw across the Rio Grande.

The second treaty between Santa Anna and Texas was kept secret. It said that Santa Anna would attempt to get the Mexican people to recognize Texas Independence and never again take up arms against them. The treaty set the Texas-Mexico border at the Rio Grande. In return for these conditions the Texans would allow Santa Anna to return to Mexico.

On May 27, 1836, Santa Anna and other prisoners were moved back to the Invincible, ready to return to Veracruz, Mexico.

Plans soon started to unravel. On June 1, 130 volunteers from New Orleans and another 120 men from across the United States arrived at Velasco, demanding Santa Anna's death. These men had not fought for Texas and were not citizens of Texas. Before long a riot was brewing in Velasco!

Santa Anna was scared for his life. When the mob demanded that he be taken off the Invincible, he threw a tantrum, saying that he was dying and was too ill to be moved and that he would never leave the ship alive.

The Ghosts of Orozimbo

President Burnet also feared for Santa Anna's safety and knew he had to get the general back to Mexico. He ordered that Santa Anna be taken off the ship and held prisoner in Quintana, across the river from Velasco. Finally on June 15, Santa Anna was moved back to Velasco and, under the supervision of Major William Patton, was put on the steamship Laura and sailed up the Brazos River for his own safety.

General Santa Anna and the poison wine

On June 16, 1836, the steamship Laura arrived at Bell's Landing, now called East Columbia. Two miles outside of Columbia was a plantation owned by Major Patton's family and so the major decided to take Santa Anna there. It is believed that Santa Anna and the other prisoners were kept for six weeks in the Race House, a wooden structure that stood on land now occupied by oil derricks.

The Patton Plantation
(Now Varner-Hogg Plantation State Historic Site)
Image courtesy of the Brazoria County Historical Museum

The Ghosts of Orozimbo

At the Patton Plantation (now known as the Varner-Hogg Plantation), Santa Anna was treated more as a guest than a prisoner, however, and he was even allowed visitors! A visit by one particular guest, though, nearly resulted in Santa Anna's death after he drank poisoned wine.

A Spanish lady living in Columbia had come to visit Santa Anna, bringing gifts of fine wine and fine food. As she was leaving, she dropped her glove at Santa Anna's feet. Major Patton, being a gentleman, picked it up and discovered a note in Spanish inside the little finger of the glove. The lady demanded the note back, unread, but Patton refused. He took the note to Vergil Phelps, Orlando Phelps' brother, because he knew some Spanish.

When the note was translated into English, Major Patton was horrified. It told Santa Anna that one of the bottles of wine had been drugged and was intended for the guards so that Santa Anna could escape. The other bottle of wine contained poison, in case the escape plan was discovered. The note also told Santa Anna that horses were waiting outside the plantation for his escape.

By the time that Patton had solved the puzzle of the Spanish note, it was too late. Santa Anna had already drunk some of the poisoned wine and was writhing around on the floor in agony, near death.

Major Patton quickly put Santa Anna in the family carriage and drove him twelve miles to Orozimbo Plantation to see Dr. James Phelps. Dr. Phelps placed Santa Anna in a large mahogany chair and used a stomach pump to save the general's life.

Many Texans wanted Santa Anna dead in revenge for the Battle of the Alamo and for the Goliad Massacre. Plots to release him and execute him had been uncovered. So Major Patton decided to keep Santa Anna at Orozimbo, which was farther up the Brazos River and more secure.

During his five months at Orozimbo, Santa Anna was treated more as a favored guest than a prisoner. He slept on the finest feather bed, ate the best food that the Phelps family could offer, and was allowed to walk freely around the plantation. He would even play games of draughts.

On one occasion a soldier guarding him tried to shoot him, but Mrs. Phelps saved his life by throwing her arms around Santa Anna to prevent the soldier from shooting!

But on August 17, 1836 the Texans got wind of a plot by the Mexicans to free Santa Anna. As a consequence, he was chained to the huge oak tree that we now call the Orozimbo Oak. The chains had been made by a blacksmith in Columbia.

Santa Anna described his feelings at the time: "I had been taken to Orozimbo where, as a result of a plan to escape from my prison by my clerk, Don Ramon Caro-as I was afterward informed-a heavy ball and chain was placed on me on the 17th of August. We wore them for 52 days."

The chains were removed during the second week of October when President Jackson agreed that Santa Anna would be allowed to go to Washington to discuss U.S.-Texas-Mexico relations.

It was reported, however, that Mrs. Almira Phelps Garrison, daughter of Orlando Phelps, remembered being told by her father that Santa Anna was never kept in chains and was never chained to the Orozimbo Oak!

Stephen F. Austin came to visit Santa Anna while he was a prisoner. They sat and talked under the huge oak tree. Some weeks later, under that same oak tree, Santa Anna tried to take poison a second time. By now the defeated and humiliated general had had several months to reflect on his failure at San Jacinto. He expected he would surely be shot as a prisoner of war by the citizens of a free Texas. He was so despondent that he managed to bribe a sympathetic servant from the Phelps household to give him poison with his food. Santa Anna was found after dinner writhing under the oak tree. Once again the Phelps family came to his recue and Dr. Phelps pumped out his stomach and saved his life.

General Santa Anna recognized the kindness of the Phelps family. When a prized family Bible was stolen from the family by Mexican soldiers, Santa Anna used his influence to have the Bible returned.

Sometime in the late fall of 1836, Mexican loyalists came up with another plan to free Santa Anna from Orozimbo. This attempt was planned for a moonless night and was said to have failed because of ghostly intervention. The story of the Hounds of Orozimbo has now become a legend.

Someone in the Phelps household loyal to Santa Anna had drugged the guards and the servants and warned Santa Anna to be ready to run. The Mexican rescuers arrived by boat in heavy rain. The dense undergrowth and many trees along the banks of the Brazos, along with the sound of the rain, helped to conceal their arrival. As they approached the house they heard a terrifying sound: the deafening baying of a pack of hounds ready to attack.

One of the servants at Orozimbo awoke from his drug-induced sleep and reported that there were only three, strange-looking, half-starved dogs. Two of them glowed translucent white and the third was an unnerving pink color that looked as though the dog had been skinned. The servant recalled that all three dogs had glazed-looking eyes.

He raised the alarm, Santa Anna's rescuers fled in terror and the dogs vanished. But even after Santa Anna returned to Mexico the dogs were still seen around the plantation on moonless nights.

The Phelps family did not own any dogs and neither did anyone who lived close by, so the dogs became known as The Ghost Dogs. It wasn't until years later, when a visitor to Orozimbo was told the story of Santa Anna's attempted rescue, that the mystery was partially solved.

The visitor recognized the dogs from the description as those belonging to a neighbor of his from Washington-on-the-Brazos, over one hundred miles away. These dogs had been very loyal to their owner and followed him everywhere. But then the neighbor left to fight for Texas Independence and was one of 309 men killed by Santa Anna at Goliad. Following his death the dogs refused to eat and seemed to sense that their master would never return.

The mystery that still remains is how the dogs ended up at Orozimbo, so far from their home, and just at the time when Santa Anna was being held prisoner.

Even today people claim to have seen two white dogs and one pink one hanging around the old Orozimbo plantation, particularly on moonless nights. And yet, Santa Anna was at Orozimbo close to two centuries ago!

General Santa Anna and the funeral for a leg!

Two years after San Jacinto, Santa Anna was again doing battle, this time with the French! His left leg was hit by cannon fire and had to be amputated. The General buried his leg with full military honors at his hacienda near Veracruz, Mexico. The leg remained buried there for four years.

On September 16, 1842 Santa Anna's supporters paraded his leg through Mexico City and reburied it in a shrine called the Pantheon of Saint Paula.

Two years later Santa Anna was overthrown and rioters stole his leg! When Santa Anna died at in 1876 at age 82, his leg had still not been found.

There are many stories about his artificial legs. His most special leg was made of wood and cork and beautifully carved. In 1847, Santa Anna and his men were taking a break during a battle near the border. Santa Anna had removed his leg to sit under a tree and eat lunch. They were suddenly attacked by the men of the 4th Illinois Infantry. Santa Anna galloped off in a hurry, forgetting his leg. He also left behind a cache of gold and a hastily abandoned meal.

The U. S. sergeant who grabbed the wooden leg travelled to county fairs and exhibited the leg for "a dime a peek!" Since 1922 it has been on display at the

Illinois State Military Museum. No one from Mexico or Texas has ever tried to kidnap it, although the Mexican government has requested on many occasions that it be returned to Mexico.

What most people don't know is that two of Santa Anna's artificial legs were captured that day in 1847 by the 4th Illinois Infantry! The second leg was just a simple peg leg that Santa Anna also left behind. Also on that day Lieutenant Sergeant Abner Doubleday gathered his men for a game of baseball just south of the border. They used Santa Anna's peg leg for a bat! This was the first recorded game of baseball ever to be played in Mexico!

General Santa Anna and Orlando Phelps

Orlando Phelps was the eldest son of Dr. James Phelps. Born in June 1822, he was away at college in Mississippi when Santa Anna was held prisoner at Orozimbo. Orlando's college roommate was Jefferson Davis, who later became president of the Confederacy. Orlando had heard his father deny on many occasions that Santa Anna had ever been chained during his stay on the plantation, but many people, including Santa Anna himself, said that he had been.

In March 1842, long after the Treaties of Velasco, Mexican troops crossed the border and attacked San Antonio, Goliad and Victoria before retreating back to Mexico.

President Houston was angered by this flagrant violation of the treaties and so in 1843 he sent General Alexander Somerville to invade Mexico in retaliation. When Somerville reached the border, Houston retracted his orders and told Somerville that the soldiers were to turn around. But 180 men, including Orlando Phelps, decided to ignore Houston's change of orders and continued across the Rio Grande and into Mexico.

On the other side of the border, the Texans attacked the town of Mier and were defeated. The 176 men who survived, including Orlando Phelps, were taken prisoner and marched to Mexico City.

There are many different accounts of what happened next. Most historians agree that Santa Anna wanted to execute all 176 prisoners. But protests from American and British ambassadors dissuaded him, and instead he ordered that every tenth man would die. This practice, known as decimation, was first used by the Roman army.

And so a jar was filled with 176 beans: 159 white beans and 17 black beans. Those men unlucky enough to draw a black bean would be executed. The young Orlando was one of those 17 who drew a black bean. He was only 20 years old at the time.

Santa Anna was given the list of men to be executed. He instantly recognized the name Phelps and ordered that the young man be brought to him at the presidential palace. He asked Orlando if he was the son of James Phelps. When Orlando replied that he was, Santa Anna offered him a deal. If Orlando swore allegiance to Mexico then he would be set free.

Orlando refused. But Santa Anna, remembering how kind Orlando's parents had been, gave Orlando $500, dressed him in fine clothing and had him escorted safely back to the border.

Orlando Phelps lived for many years at Orozimbo after his parents died. Of his five children, Almira Phelps was his youngest daughter. He died in August 1897, at the age of 75. His official grave is in

The Ghosts of Orozimbo

Glenwood cemetery in Houston, Texas. However, many people believe that he is actually buried next to his father at Orozimbo.

General Santa Anna's later years

From 1846 to 1847 Santa Anna suffered further defeats in the Mexican-American War. He declared himself president once again, but was unsuccessful in fighting off the American invasion.

In 1848 he went into exile in Kingston, Jamaica and two years later moved to Cuba. However, in 1853 he retook the Mexican government and declared himself president for the final time. He named himself "Most Serene Highness" and declared that he was dictator-for-life. His government once again was disastrous and he was overthrown. Fearing for his life, Santa Anna fled back to Cuba. The Mexican government tried him for treason in Mexico without his being present and the Mexican government claimed all of his land.

Santa Anna spent his exile in Cuba, New York, Colombia and St. Thomas. In 1874, the Mexican government issued an amnesty, and Santa Anna, crippled and almost blind, returned to Mexico City. He died two years later, in 1876 at the age of 82.

Part 3.

Where

was

Orozimbo?

Where was Orozimbo?

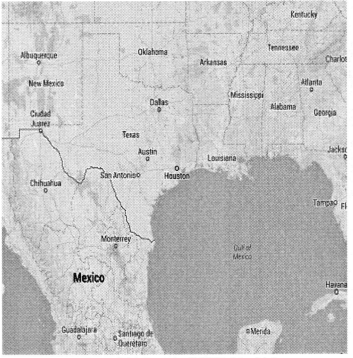

Copyright Google, INEGI, MapLink

Orozimbo Plantation was located nine miles northwest of Angleton, within the Houston metropolitan area, in Brazoria County, Texas. The old cotton plantation was built on a bend in the beautiful Brazos River. The plantation is said to have been over 130 acres when the Phelps family owned the property. But the land has now been divided up and sold to private owners.

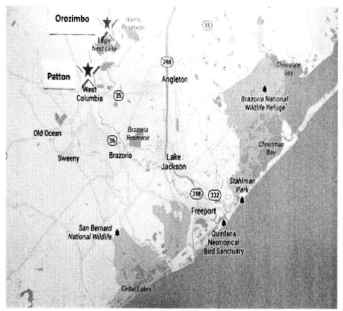

Map data 2013 copyright Google

In 1836, following several demonstrations demanding Santa Anna's death, President Burnet knew that the general's life was in danger. On June 15 Major William Patton and his men put Santa Anna on the steamship, Laura, and they sailed up the Brazos River from Freeport to West Columbia. On June 16, at 11 a.m., they disembarked at Bells Landing, now known as East Columbia, and Santa Anna was taken to the Patton Plantation two miles northwest of Columbia.

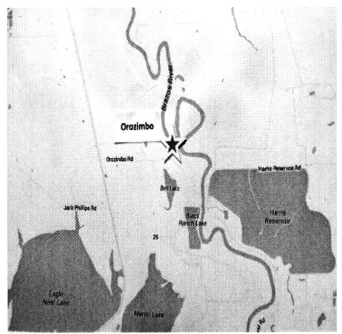

Map data 2013 copyright Google

After a plot to rescue Santa Anna was uncovered, he was moved to Orozimbo Plantation, farther up the Brazos River. Santa Anna was held at Orozimbo from July 30, 1836 until November 26, 1836, when David G. Burnet, President of the newly formed Republic of Texas, gave him permission to travel to Washington, D.C.

Sources

Maps/Plans/Photographs

Photographs of Orozimbo Plantation, courtesy of Brazoria County Historical Museum

Photograph of historical marker at Orozimbo, courtesy of Brazoria County Historical Museum

Photograph of Varner-Hogg Plantation, courtesy of Brazoria County Historical Museum

Photographs taken by H.J. Ralles

Public Domain photographs and painting of Santa Anna

Map data copyright 2013 Google

Articles

"Santa Anna Imprisoned Here," *The Brazosport Facts*, June 6, 1976. No author credited.

"Plantation Prison," *The Brazosport Facts*, July 22, 1979. No author credited.

Emma Elliot, "Huge historical tree destroyed by fire at Orozimbo Plantation," *The Brazosport Facts*, January 28, 1981.

Michael Wright, "The Tribulations of Santa Anna," *The Brazosport Facts*, August 2000.

Rick Barrick, "Local Landmarks," *The Brazosport Facts*, Date?

"Nephew Of The Man Who Saved Santa Anna's Life Relates Account Of Capture," *The Houston Chronicle*, April 27, 1929. No author credited.

Catherine Munson, "Santa Anna Spared Youth In Mier Invasion Whose Father Saved His Life After Defeat," *The Houston Chronicle*, February 24, 1929

Maxey Brooks, "Santa Anna in Brazoria County," Maxey's Musings, Date?

Tom Davison, "Santa Anna's "Suicide"," The Family Saga by Abernathy, Texas Folklore Society.

"Santa Anna at the Phelps Plantation," as told to Jamie Giesecke by Mrs. Mary Kennedy Giessecke of Angleton, Texas, December 18, 1966.

Websites

The Handbook of Texas Online: Phelps, James Aeneas, E.
http://www.tshaonline.org/handbook/online/articles/fph02

Varner Hogg Plantation, State Historic Site
http://www.visitvarnerhoggplantation.com/index.aspx?page=19

Captured Leg of Santa Anna, Springfield, Illinois-Roadside America
http://www.roadsideamerica.com/story/18808

Fairweather Lewis, The Hounds of Orozimbo
http://fairweatherlewis.wordpress.com/2010/10/21/the-hounds-of-orozimbo/

History of Us, Antonio Lopez de Santa Anna, His Wooden Leg, and the Beginning of Baseball in Mexico
http://votto1234.blogspot.com/2010/10/antonio-lopez-de-santa-anna-his-wooden.html

Gary McKee, Drumroll!
http://www.dailyyonder.com/drumroll/2009/10/02/2377

Wikipedia, Antonio Lopez de Santa Anna
http://en.wikipedia.org/wiki/Antonio_L%C3%B3pez_de_Santa_Anna

Orlando C. Phelps-World Connect Project
http://wc.rootsweb.ancestry.com/cgi-bin/igm.cgi?op=GET&db=i
mccriv&id=I3533

Find a Grave, Orlando C. Phelps

About the Author

Photo taken by the Tribune Newspaper, Humble, Texas

H.J. Ralles is a teacher who turned to writing books for children in 1997. Originally from the United Kingdom, H.J. Ralles has lived in the United States since 1990 and now lives in Huffman, Texas. She is the author of Look Out Of My Window, a picture book for younger readers, the popular Keeper series and three other science fiction novels for 9- to 14-year-olds. The Ghosts of Orozimbo is the long-awaited sequel to The Ghosts of Malhado.

To learn more about H.J. Ralles visit:
www.hjralles.com